Ten Days with Sasquatch

J.E. Brown

PublishAmerica
Baltimore

ISBN: 1-4241-7056-7
PUBLISHED BY PUBLISHAMERICA, LLLP
www.publishamerica.com
Baltimore

Printed in the United States of America

This book is dedicated to my children,
Emily & James
"Reach for the stars and become one"

Chapter One

Friday, October 13, 2006
Day 1

The view from the campsite looked like a picture on the front of a postcard. The dew on the trees glistened, like diamonds through the early morning sunrise. All the green was fading from the landscape and turning to the brown and gray that was synonymous with autumn. The air was fresh and cold and Bo could see the mist from his breath as he exhaled the warm air stored deep in his chest.

Bo, who was twenty-nine, loved the outdoors and felt right at home there. He was five feet, eleven inches tall with dark hair and a dark five o'clock shadow for a beard. He had spent a lot of time camping and hunting, but this was his first trip to the Modoc National Forest. He had moved to southern Oregon a year earlier and couldn't wait to hit the snowcapped mountains of northern California. He had also spent eight years in the army and knew how to live off the land. His experiences in the army included a stint in Afghanistan, which he often said would be a great place to visit if it weren't for all the bullets that kept flying by.

Bo called JT three days earlier and asked him if he wanted to join him on this camping trip. JT didn't hesitate to say yes, although he should have, because Sarah, his girlfriend, wasn't too happy about the idea. She was the type that had her feet planted firmly on the ground. A high school teacher in southern Oregon, she was ready to settle down and start a family. Sarah didn't like it when Bo would call out of the blue and convince JT to join him on some escapade in the wild. JT had often mentioned how Bo had once saved his life in Afghanistan and just felt like he owed him. But in reality, he loved it when Bo called. It always meant some kind of adventure.

They invited Sarah as well, but she didn't want to miss an entire week of work to go, so she resigned herself to the idea of being without him, like she always did. This time, he would be gone for ten days, unlike the weekend trips they usually took. It would be a good time for her as well, she thought.

The two men set out for their trip on Thursday morning at five a.m. and arrived at their destination about seven p.m., after a five-and-a-half-hour hike, where they found the perfect campsite. The campsite was situated on top of a hill that sat about thirty yards from a creek bed that wound itself through the forest. The three tents could barely be seen with their camouflaged design. A thick blanket of trees ran alongside the tents. There was a small opening in the tree line where the tents were set up in a triangular formation.

A campfire from the night before still smoldered and a

light plume of smoke arose from the charred logs. The fire had brought some needed warmth the night before.

JT was still asleep and Bo was taking in the beauty of the land that Mother Nature was seemingly showing off to him. He could see the top of the mountain range that seemed to disappear over the horizon as he looked off to the west. Bo finally decided that he couldn't keep all this to himself and went over to wake JT.

"Hey, buddy. Rise and shine. Time to get up." JT didn't move. Bo decided to use a tactic that they were both familiar with from their days in the army together. Bo reached down and grabbed the corners of JT's sleeping bag and pulled hard until JT fell completely out and Bo was holding the bag in his hands, like the drill sergeant used to do back in basic training. JT jumped up as if his tent were on fire.

"What the hell?" JT stammered in his half awake and half asleep state of mind. Bo began to laugh and JT didn't see the humor in it at all, but it didn't take long for a halfhearted smile to creep across JT's face.

JT stood, stretching his arms high above his head and gave a good, hardy morning yawn. "Dude," Bo said, "you've got to check this place out."

The two men walked down to the creek bed and stood in amazement as they looked over the area, while JT whispered in a low voice that sounded as if he couldn't speak at all.

"This is incredible." JT, like Bo, loved the outdoors and could appreciate the sheer beauty of what he was looking at. JT repeated himself louder this time and said, "This is incredible."

Bo broke up the moment by saying, "Yes, it is, but we still need to get firewood, water and food."

The two men left behind the view and walked back towards the campsite. Bo started to gather the wood while JT set off down the dry creek bed to find some clean, fresh water.

It was an hour later when JT arrived with the water. Bo had already gathered up enough firewood to last at least two or three days and had piled it up neatly against a tree that sat about fifteen feet away from the campfire.

"How far is it to the water?" Bo asked.

JT replied, "Well, not really too far." JT paused. There was…" He paused again. "I'm not sure, a bear or a mountain lion, I guess. Something was there and that's all I know."

"Did you see it?" Bo asked, with a look of excitement in his eyes.

"I think I would know the difference between a bear and a mountain lion if I had seen it," JT replied, with a hint of laughter in his voice. "All I know for sure," he continued, "is something was watching me. I could feel it… It was weird.

JT, who served with Bo for the last three years in the army, usually wasn't shaken up too easily. He stood about six feet two inches tall and was built solid. He wore a small scar over his right eye that he had earned while in the army. He had blond hair and blue eyes and a baby face to match.

Bo looked over and noticed that JT was standing facing the curve in the creek bed that wandered around the bend and out of sight. He just seemed to be staring into space. Something had gotten into his head. Bo broke his concentration by waving his hand up and down in front of JT's eyes.

"Come on, man, what was it?" Bo asked.

"I'm really not sure," JT said. "But there are a lot of things out there that it could have been and I'm sure it was nothing to worry about. Now, how about some breakfast?"

Bo had already rekindled the fire and laid out some bacon and eggs to cook up for breakfast. It was their first meal in what was to be their new home for the next ten days. And it wasn't long before both men were stretched out in the grass, letting their food digest.

Neither was talking until Bo said out of the blue, "Maybe it was Bigfoot."

JT just shook his head and said, "Yeah, right." And that's all that was said for the next hour or so.

"Well, Mr. Leader," JT finally broke the silence and asked, "what's on our agenda for today?"

"I was thinking about going over that ridge," Bo replied, "and checking it out today."

"Let's do it," JT said, as he got to his feet.

The two men grabbed their backpacks and started towards the ridge that looked to be only a couple of miles away. They cut up and joked around a lot while hiking, but that all ended as they approached the ridge.

"The view here is even better than the one at the campsite," Bo said.

JT agreed as they stood overlooking the view of the most amazing mountain range they had ever seen.

"Come on," Bo yelled, "I'll race you to the bottom." He started to run while JT followed closely.

The forest seemed to swallow them up as they ran.

There weren't any paths and they were in an area not many people had ever seen before. And that's exactly what they were looking for.

JT pulled ahead as they reached the edge of a stream at the bottom of the ridge.

"You cheated," Bo yelled. "You grabbed me and slowed me down."

Laughing, JT just said, "Don't get mad at me because you're slow."

They reached into their packs and pulled out some string and hooks. And while Bo rounded up some sticks to use as fishing rods, JT went looking for bait.

Bo could hear JT rustling around in the woods, but to his surprise, JT came out from a different location than where the sounds were coming from. Bo stood motionless as he scanned the woods for the source of the sound.

JT, unaware of the noise, was asking if Bo was ready to get lunch. JT found some worms under a piece of a log that had fallen from a tree and was partially decayed. He stopped in his tracks when he realized that Bo had not heard a word he said, but was scanning the tree line.

JT started looking in the same direction that Bo seemed to be entranced in.

"What is it? Did you see something? Where did it go?" JT was asking. Bo just put his finger slowly to his lips, silently asking JT to keep it down.

By now JT was standing next to Bo looking in the same direction and asked, "What are we looking for?"

Bo explained what he had heard and how he thought it was JT until he came from the other direction.

"Maybe it's our Bigfoot," JT joked, as he nudged Bo in the arm with his elbow.

"Yeah, I'm sure it is," Bo said half joking, but now he thought there may be some truth to it.

They started fishing and forgot about the noise until they saw a splash in the water just a few feet away from where they were standing.

"What the hell was that?" Bo yelled as he turned toward the wooded area again. JT stood motionless and didn't really want to look, but did anyway.

"You think someone is playing games with us?" JT asked.

"Like who? Who would be all the way out here?" Bo snapped back.

"Well, we are," JT said as if looking for the best explanation.

"Look," Bo said, "we've caught enough fish for lunch and dinner; let's just get the hell out of here."

"I'm with ya," JT responded without any hesitation. The hike back to camp was uneventful.

By now it was already early afternoon. As the men were cleaning the fish, Bo spoke up and said, "Look, I have to tell you something."

"What?" JT asked. JT could tell by the sound of Bo's voice that he really didn't want to hear this.

"Well," Bo said, "I kind of had a feeling we would run into something out here." JT's face hardened, but he didn't say anything. "Look, the real reason I wanted to come out here is because I've been following the recent sightings of Bigfoot in this area."

"Come on, Bo. Get real. You know better than that," JT snapped.

"No, listen," Bo calmly said. "There have been four sightings about seven or eight miles from here in just the past few days. I wanted to see if we could get it on film. I know you're skeptical of all those things, like UFOs, Loch Ness, Bigfoot, and all that kind of stuff, so I was hoping that once I got you out here, you would understand and help me out. We can be rich, really rich…you know, loaded."

"Wait a second," JT interrupted. "You mean to tell me you brought me on some wild goose chase and didn't think it was important enough to tell me?"

"I know what you're thinking," Bo said. "You're thinking I'm nuts. But come on, man, what was watching you earlier and what was making those sounds in the woods? And even more so, what the hell threw that rock at us while we were fishing?"

"I don't have the answers, but I bet they make perfect sense," JT said. "The noises we heard were just wild animals and the rock probably wasn't even a rock. I bet it was a fish jumping. And if it was a Bigfoot," JT continued, "how do you plan to find it when no one else can seem to get it on film?"

"Good question, JT." Bo was smiling now because he knew he had piqued JT's interest in this thing.

"Here's what I have planned. Last year when Mom and Dad died, it really made me think about my life. I know I'm here for a reason and this is it. I took most of the money from the inheritance and bought some simple equipment that I brought with us. Look at this." Bo walked over to the tent and JT followed. "I have a camera that has night vision and a small camcorder that we can keep on us all the time. And I got one for you, too."

"You mean to tell me that you carried all that equipment the whole way?"

"Yeah, but it's small and compact stuff. It only added a few pounds to my pack and the extra batteries were the heaviest part. Look, give me a few days and if you want to leave, we will."

JT stood silent for a few minutes. He pondered the thought of teaching Bo a lesson about spending all his money and running off on a wild goose chase, but on the other hand, what if Bigfoot was out there and really did exist? They could be rich just for getting one piece of footage. And how hard could that be, he wondered.

He looked back at Bo and asked, "How rich?"

Bo reached out and grabbed JT by the hand and pulled him in for a hug and said, "Beyond your wildest dreams. You and Sarah can get married and raise a family and you wouldn't even have to work."

JT loved his job as a freelance computer programmer and insisted he wasn't giving up his job. He was able to take off all the time he wanted and didn't have to answer to anyone—but Sarah, of course.

JT agreed to the hunt and Bo began telling him of his plan and how he hadn't expected to run into one so early.

"Look, the four sightings were towards the north," Bo explained, "and the first was farther north than the second and the second farther than the third, and so on and so on. What we need to do is get set up and go from there."

"Yep," JT said, "this is a half-baked idea," but he listened on.

"We need to look for evidence that he's here in this area and then hunt him. We don't have to kill him or even shoot him. There's only been one reported death at the hands of Bigfoot. We are safe out here, no matter how scared you are."

Bo explained that Teddy Roosevelt had mentioned a death by a Bigfoot attack in a book he had written in 1890 called *The Wilderness Hunter*.

"Look, Bo," JT interrupted. "Do you think that the reason there's only been one death mentioned could be because when it warns people, they usually listen and get the hell away from it?"

Bo looked surprised by the question and realized it was a good one.

"Come on, man. How many people out there have our training for this terrain and can move as fast as we can around it?"

JT smiled and said, "Listen, I'm in, but I'm not going to put my life or yours on the line just for that perfect shot. So what do we do first to get a shot at this so-called monster?"

"Well, we need to find out where it feeds, I guess," Bo replied.

JT smiled and said, "This is just great. Here we are in the middle of nowhere, with no experience with this matter, and you're guessing what to do first."

Bo explained some of the things he had read on the Internet about deer being found missing only the liver, so they decided with only about four hours of daylight left that that's what they would start looking for, deer carcasses.

They decided to split up and look so they could cover more ground, but were careful not to get too far from each other. Their search came up empty.

The night closed in fast around them and all they had for light was the campfire they had made the night before that they managed to keep going and two lanterns that they had brought with them. While sitting around the campfire talking about their army days and girls they had conquered, they seemingly forgot about Bigfoot until they heard a loud, brisk howling coming from deep in the darkness. They both seemed to turn to stone without even so much as turning their heads in that direction. They listened intently to the cries from the woods.

Bo slowly turned to JT and asked, "How far away would you say it is?"

JT replied, "It's probably a wolf and it seems to be close to the stream we were fishing earlier."

"It's not a wolf and you know it," Bo responded.

"Look, Bo," JT said, "I'm still not convinced that some creature wanders the woods. I admit that I'm not sure what it is, but that doesn't mean it's Bigfoot."

The howling went on for another twenty to twenty-five minutes and then it stopped. The one thing they noticed was that while the howling was going on, nothing else made a sound, not even the crickets.

A few minutes after the howling had stopped Bo asked, "So how do you want to handle the sleeping schedule? Maybe in four-hour shifts?" he continued.

"Well," JT responded, "we will lose a lot of daylight that way. Let's just both go to bed for now and if something happens, then tomorrow we can try something else."

"Sounds fine to me," Bo said, "but I'm sleeping with one eye open all night."

At around two a.m. both men were awakened by something smashing into their tents.

JT screamed from his tent to Bo, "What the hell was that?"

Bo sat and listened to the objects hit the tent and the ground around the tent. "Okay, skeptic," Bo yelled back, "what kind of animals throw rocks and things at people?" Bo asked as if to be saying, *I told you so.*

JT slowly unzipped his tent just enough to peek outside and what he saw would forever stay in his mind. JT was looking at something that had to be at least eight feet tall or seemed to be. All he could see was a silhouette standing about twenty feet from the campsite and it was throwing objects underhanded towards them.

He turned quickly to grab the camera, but the creature was gone before he could aim it. The bombardment was over, at least for now.

Both Bo and JT were standing outside the tent in just a few seconds after it was over. Using their lanterns, they could see pine cones all over their campsite.

The look on JT's face was a look of horror as Bo began to ask what he saw.

JT looked at Bo and all he could say at the moment was, "I tried to get the camera, but it was gone."

"What was gone?" Bo questioned. "Did you see it?"

JT looked at Bo and said, "That damn thing is huge. Holy Cow, it was huge."

About that time the howling began again, and this time it was coupled with a pounding sound as if someone was hitting a tree with a baseball bat. They listened for about half an hour, and then it stopped. Neither man got any more sleep during the night. Bo spent the rest of the night with the night vision camera panning the area and JT sat in total amazement over what had just taken place and what he had seen with his own eyes.

Could there really have been some creature standing there or were his eyes playing tricks on him? He tried to tell himself it was just a tree, but he knew better. JT had seen Bigfoot with his own eyes and was now a believer.

Chapter Two

As the sunlight filled the forest, the two men could now see the mess made by their visitor in the darkness of night. Pine cones laid spread around the entire campsite.

Bo looked at JT and asked if he thought maybe there was more than one. JT sat down on a log and just shook his head. The visions of what he saw the night before filled his mind like a cup running over with water.

He looked at Bo and replied, "If there is more than one of those things out there, I'm leaving now!"

Bo sat down next to him and asked if he was okay. And JT started explaining what he saw in the light of the moon last night.

"Man, that thing was huge. It has really long arms and was looking right at me. I mean, I couldn't see its face, but it was looking right at me. I could feel its stare. It was only pine cones last night, but it could have been worse. It could have been logs or giant rocks. We could have been killed!"

"Look, JT," Bo said, "if that thing wanted us dead, it would have killed us. I don't think they are violent creatures. I think all it was trying to do was scare us."

"And it worked," replied JT.

"If we can get set up tonight, then it can't sneak up on us. Then we will have a tactical advantage," explained Bo. "All we need to do is..."

They heard a noise in the brush and something was coming right toward them. The men scrambled to their feet and ran to hide in a row of trees behind the tents. They listened as the sounds got closer and closer. Their hearts were pounding. Bo realized he didn't have his camera and sprinted to the supply tent to retrieve it. JT just stood motionless as he watched Bo and scanned the tree line. He felt concern for his friend, but knew if the creature attacked now, there was nothing he could do but watch.

Bo made it to the tent and grabbed the camera. He spun to face the tree line, where the noise was coming from. The rustling in the woods continued. Bo sprinted back to his original hiding place and aimed his camera towards the noise and waited. They waited for what seemed like hours but, in reality, was only seconds. Suddenly something just burst out of the woods.

It wasn't the creature they expected at all; it was a woman. Then just a couple seconds later, a young man popped out as well. The couple was shocked as Bo and JT walked out from behind the row of trees in which they were hiding.

"You guys scared the hell out of us," JT said with a smile on his face.

"We're so sorry for intruding; we didn't realize

anyone else was up here." The woman sounded very apologetic. She was attractive, about five foot six, with dark hair.

Bo walked over to them and made an introduction. "Hi, my name is Bo and this is my friend JT." He reached out to shake the man's hand.

The young man smiled and responded, "My name is Todd and this is my sister, Jenny," as he shook Bo's hand.

"So," Jenny said, with a smile on her face, "what were you guys afraid of?"

JT started to explain, but Bo cut him off and said, "We weren't really scared of anything in particular, we just though maybe you were a bear." Jenny looked him and Bo and he could tell she wasn't buying it.

"You two on vacation?" he asked.

Todd looked at Bo and said, "Not really a vacation, just a weekend getaway."

Jenny, who was still studying Bo, asked him about his camera.

Bo laughed and replied, "Well, if a bear did come out, it would make some good footage from our trip." And again, Bo could tell she wasn't buying it.

JT broke up the stale moment and asked if Todd and Jenny were hungry and explained that they were just about to start breakfast.

Todd and Jenny accepted. During breakfast Todd and Jenny learned that Bo and JT were army buddies and that JT had a girlfriend back home who didn't want to join them. And Bo and JT learned that Todd and Jenny made the trip up yesterday morning.

"Where's your campsite?" JT asked.

"It's about three miles to the south. We went out this morning to see if we could find whatever was screaming last night." Todd further explained that his sister was a Bigfoot enthusiast and dragged him up here because she didn't want to be by herself.

JT looked over at Bo because he knew their story was almost the same, but he was deceived in going on the trip.

Jenny was looking over the campsite when she asked about the pine cones spread throughout. Bo decided that if she were a Bigfoot enthusiast, as Todd said, then she obviously knew more about Bigfoot than he did.

"Okay, look," Bo said, "last night we had an encounter." He emphasized the word "encounter" while motioning quotations with his fingers. "Something was throwing these pine cones at us last night." He pointed at JT and said, "He saw it in the tree line, but I didn't see anything, but I know something was there."

Jenny moved closer to the edge of the rock she was using as a chair and with excitement in her voice asked, "You saw it?" All of her concentration was on JT.

JT, still noticeably shaken, said, "All I can tell you is that this thing is big, I mean real big, and it had long arms, kind of like they didn't go with that body. All I saw was the silhouette and I could feel it looking at me."

"Did you smell anything?" Jenny asked.

"Yeah," Bo cut in. "There was a terrible smell."

"Wow, this is so exciting," she said. "You guys had a real encounter."

JT looked at Jenny and asked her if she thought it would come back. She smiled and said, "I hope so."

Todd had seemed to hear enough. "You guys aren't

really sure what you saw, are you? I mean, it could have been a bear, right?"

Jenny looked at Todd with a stern look as if to say, *Be quiet.*

Todd stood up and walked down by the creek bed. Jenny apologized for Todd and explained that the only reason he was here was to prove her wrong. And she could tell he didn't like the fact that something just might be out there.

The three continued to talk for the next several minutes until Todd started yelling, "You guys had better come down here quick and check this out!"

The three made their way down to where Todd was standing. They found Todd standing over two complete sets of tracks, one heading to the campsite and one going away! Jenny quickly pulled out a tape measure from a pocket on her jacket and measured the print.

"Seventeen and three-quarters of an inch long," she exclaimed.

The tracks coming in were about six feet apart and the ones leaving were even further apart, which led them to believe that it walked into, and ran out of the campsite.

They went back to the campsite with the new evidence and sat around the fire talking about what this showed and what they were going to do next.

They decided that Todd and Jenny would move their campsite and join Bo and JT.

So, they all hiked to Todd and Jenny's site, packed up and moved everything to Bo and JT's campsite, where they set up and made one larger campsite.

Jenny was still fascinated with what JT had seen the night before and questioned him often about his sighting.

But JT still only gave vague answers because he, himself, wasn't sure what he saw and couldn't explain it any better.

By now, it was early afternoon and the plan was to set up the equipment that Jenny had with her, which was more sophisticated than Bo's. They had already found footprints in the mud and Jenny was going to make a couple of cast molds out of the better footprints.

Bo, JT and Todd started setting up sound and video equipment that Jenny and Todd brought with them.

With two cameras set up, one on the campsite and one overlooking the creek bed, and all four armed with a small camcorder, they set out to see if they could track where the giant had gone.

They followed a few tracks and some broken branches for several miles, when they made a gruesome discovery of three dead deer lying spread out in a small opening in the heavy brush.

Each deer had a broken leg, which was evident by the way the legs were contorted. They also noticed that each deer had a hole in their belly with the guts half pulled out. Jenny searched the carcass of each deer, and noticed that the only thing missing was the liver!

JT couldn't understand why only the liver was gone and why it didn't eat the muscle and the fat that was still left, which had obvious nutritional value.

He then remembered what Bo had told him as Jenny explained that there had been numerous discoveries of deer found in this same manner and went on to explain that the liver contains all the vitamins needed to support life, especially vitamin A.

They took lots of pictures and used up some film on their discovery and moved on. They felt as though they had all the evidence needed to assure them that this was a Bigfoot and not some other animal, like a bear or mountain lion.

As they searched through the woods, they found that there were no more tacks and that there was no more proof that the creature had traveled this far.

The group decided to take a different route back to camp so they could maybe pick up new tracks or evidence showing that the Bigfoot had been in the area.

The hike back to camp was over some pretty treacherous terrain and not easily traveled. The group had to rest for a few minutes so they found rocks and old logs to sit on.

No one talked for the first several minutes. Then Todd broke the silence and asked, "So, what if we do find this thing? Then what?"

JT seconded the question with, "Yeah, then what?" Bo looked at Jenny with a look of confusion and said, "All I wanted was to film it. I didn't expect it to bomb our campsite with pine cones."

Jenny stood and said, "If we get it on film, then we're famous. None of us would ever have to work again."

Bo shook his head in agreement and added, "And that's just with one piece of footage on film. Can you imagine if we could kill one or even catch one alive?"

Jenny quickly interrupted him saying, "I don't know what your plan is, but I don't think killing or catching one alive is going to happen out here."

Bo stood and said, "Look, it's simple. We set a trap and try to cripple one, not kill, just cripple."

JT, seeming very agitated, jumped up and reminded Bo that he was the only one to see the Bigfoot, Sasquatch, or whatever this thing was and he could tell by the sheer size and strength that a normal trap like the ones they made in the army was not going to cripple it—or even slow it down, for that matter.

Bo turned to him and snapped back with, "You are the only one who saw it and you can't say anything about it but it was huge."

JT sat back down and put his head in his hands and just said again, "It was huge."

The group rested quietly for about ten more minutes and started back to camp. The rest of their hike was uneventful until they reached camp and quickly realized that their friend from the night before had paid them another visit. It was long gone now, but had definitely been there.

JT's tent had been ripped out of the ground and thrown down towards the creek bed. The firewood Bo had so neatly stacked against a tree had been thrown around the campsite. And the supply tent had a giant rip in the side, where the cooler storing their food was now lying empty.

Todd yelled in anger, "Oh, man, this is just great. We have no food and now we don't have a supply tent."

Jenny seemed to be happy and Bo and JT just watched her as she ran to the supply tent, where the recordings would be from the cameras they had placed earlier. When they realized what she was so happy about, they too got very excited.

JT was looking forward to having what Bo had brought him out here to get so they could get the hell out of there. But the look on Jenny's face changed from happy and ecstatic to one of dismay and failure.

She turned to Todd and asked, "Did you forget to do something?"

Todd looked back confused and replied, "What do you mean?"

"The cameras, dummy. You forgot to turn on the recorders!"

Everyone just stood in utter silence.

Todd, after thinking about it for a moment, replied, "I thought you only wanted to run them at night."

"No," she screamed back. "Anytime we leave the campsite we need to have it on."

"Okay, fine, I screwed up," he snapped back. "Let's just pack up and go home."

JT lifted his head quickly and agreed it sounded like a plan to him. Bo stepped between Todd and Jenny, who were by now only a few feet apart and arguing about what to do now.

Bo, who was addressing Todd, said, "Look how close we are to getting exactly what we came here to get. All we need to do is stay calm and realize how lucky we really are that it came back."

"Lucky?" Todd, who was by now very agitated, responded. "Lucky? Are you kidding me? Look at what it did. What if we were still here? It probably would have killed us."

"No, it wouldn't have killed us," Bo interjected. "If it wanted to kill us, it would have done it last night. And what I mean by lucky is that it's still in the area." Then Bo quickly added, "We still have a chance to film it. Everyone just needs to calm down and relax."

"We have everything under control," Jenny added.

The camp seemed to be divided into two groups. JT and Todd, who wanted to pack up and go, and Bo and Jenny, who didn't. What they did agree on was that it would start getting dark soon and no one was leaving tonight.

They all sat in front of the fire and talked about what they would do tomorrow. Bo and Jenny talked JT and Todd into staying a little longer. After all, it did make sense that if it wanted to hurt or even kill them, it would have done so the night before.

"Tomorrow, the one thing we have got to do is get food," Bo stated.

"What do you have in mind?" Jenny asked.

"Well, if Sasquatch can catch a deer, then so can we, and it will give us something to bait it with."

"The liver," she said. "Good idea, but how do you catch a deer?" Bo walked over to his tent and retrieved a crossbow he packed for the trip. "JT and I have crossbows and in the morning, we'll go hunting. If he's still around here hunting them, then there should be more. And just in case we don't get one, Todd can go fishing. We are bound to get something if we use the resources that Mother Nature has given us."

Jenny smiled. "Well," she said, "that will give me a chance to set up the equipment again after he rummaged through the tent."

Before the day had seen the last of light, Bo and JT set out to catch something quick for dinner. They unfortunately didn't have any luck, so the group ate a trail mix that Jenny had packed and carried with her.

The temperature began to drop and darkness fell

upon the campsite. The group was hungry and cold. They decided that JT would bunk with Bo until they had time to set his tent back up in the morning.

The night began to fill with the sounds of the woods. It wasn't long until Bo and JT were fast asleep. Todd fell asleep soon after and Jenny was the only one awake when the distant thumping sounds began to fill the night. She quickly awoke Bo and the two sat quietly for a while, listening to the sounds.

"What is it?" Bo asked.

Jenny explained that she had read about the Bigfoot and how he would bang on trees, she guessed to intimidate whatever was in their territory. She said that she heard they were territorial, but that's all she really knew. The sounds went on for about an hour or so.

Bo and Jenny continued to talk for a while after the sounds had stopped. It was their first real opportunity to get to know one another. Bo learned that her parents had passed a few years earlier in a plane crash over southern California.

"That's awful," he said. "Mine were killed in an automobile crash last year."

"I'm sure you miss them," she said softly.

"Yeah, in fact it was their money I used to buy the equipment that I brought up here. Man, I had no idea what I was getting myself into."

"You got to be kidding," she said, assuring him that he was doing the right thing. "You've already had an encounter and you seemed to know right where to go to find him."

With a little laugh, he said, "Yeah, I got lucky." The two went to bed shortly after and the rest of the night passed without incident.

Chapter Three

Sunday, October 15, 2006
Day 3

The group awoke to find everything still in place. And there didn't seem to be any evidence of visitors in the night. The forest was full of the sounds that draw thousands of people a year to remote locations just like this one. But on this particular day, the wind had picked up and the air seemed a little colder.

After setting the supply tent back up, JT, fearing that water was all they were going to have today, picked up all the flasks and started heading towards the curve in the creek bed, when he heard Bo calling for him. He stopped and turned to find Bo jogging towards him.

"Nobody goes alone," Bo said, as he reached out to help carry the flasks.

JT smiled and said, "Okay, buddy, let's go." Nervous about what had happened a couple of days ago when he made this trip alone, JT was glad Bo was going with him. The men walked towards the bend and disappeared into the brush.

J.E. BROWN

The fire from the night before had all but gone out, so Jenny was getting the fire started again while Todd was rounding up some extra firewood. When Todd had an armful, he returned and started putting the wood on the fire, that was by now burning pretty good.

"You like him, don't you?" Todd asked.

Jenny, with a surprised look on her face, looked over and asked, "Like who?"

"Oh, come on, sis. I can tell when you look at him."

Jenny tilted her head a little and responded with, "Maybe. He is kind of cute and we do seem to have a lot in common. But I've only known him for one day, so let's wait awhile before you start to marry me off."

Todd laughed while saying, "I can't believe you even said the word 'marry.'"

Jenny blushed as she turned towards the supply tent and walked away.

Bo and JT walked the creek bed for about fifteen minutes, when they came upon a deep section of the creek that was filled with clean water, unlike the muddy water they had seen during the entire walk there.

"What do you make of them?" JT asked.

Bo looked confused. "What do I make of who?"

"Todd and Jenny, who else?"

"Well," Bo answered, "Todd seems like a good kid and Jenny sure is easy to look at. I guess I don't understand the question."

JT smiled. "Sure you do, you just answered it."

"Are you asking me if I like Jenny?" Bo looked up from his chore with a half smile.

JT replied, "Well, you can see it when you two look at

30

each other. Come on, man, I'm just saying you don't have the best track record with women. You haven't been in a serious relationship, ever, that I know of."

Bo stood up now that all the flasks were full and looked at JT and said, "Yeah, you're right. I'm not good with women more than one night, but she has the potential to make it a little longer. But I don't even know if she feels the same way." Bo smiled and patted JT on the back and said, "Let's go get us some deer." And the two men walked back to camp.

"Wow, that fire looks great," JT yelled as they turned the bend heading into camp.

"Well, we owe it all to Jenny," Todd responded. "She had it going before I could even get enough wood to build it."

Bo made it a point to walk over to Jenny and thank her personally for everything she'd done over the past day.

"Is everyone hungry?" Bo asked to try to rally the group. There did seem to be some extra enthusiasm as Bo went to his tent to grab some clothes to wear on their big hunt. When he found what he needed, Bo and JT suited up in their old camos, grabbed up their crossbows and headed out to catch what they hoped would be breakfast, lunch, and dinner. Not to mention, bait!

The two men were skilled with their weapons and it didn't take long before they came across a large buck.

Bo looked at JT and whispered, "It's all yours."

JT nodded and raised his crossbow and took careful aim, knowing that the next one might not be so easy to find, and fired a bolt deep into the buck's side.

Bo congratulated him on an excellent shot.

The buck staggered and ran off into the woods. They

tracked it for about half an hour when they found it lying in some deep, thorny brush.

"Wow," said JT, "that's a big buck."

"Yep," said Bo. "Now all we have to do is dig it out of there so we can eat."

The two men began to pull the brush aside so there was room next to the buck for them to sit next to it and clean it. Bo pulled out a knife and began to get the much-needed food from the dead animal. Then he lifted the ribs and began to look for the liver.

When he was done, he looked at JT and said, "I never realized how big the liver was on a deer. Can you believe this thing?"

JT just shook his head. "Think about this, as big as the liver is, do you think it would fill the Bigfoot up?"

"I'm sure it would," Bo answered.

"Then why," JT asked, "were there three dead deer with broken necks, legs, and missing livers?" He paused for a moment and finished. "There's more than one!"

Bo wondered if what JT just said could be true.

"Maybe he just stores the liver for later," Bo questioned.

"It's cold enough at night to keep the liver cold," JT said, "but not during the day and I doubt they have ice."

Bo realized that what JT was saying made perfect sense. There had to be more than one and if there was, then this trip just got a lot more dangerous. They gathered up the bounty they had taken from the dead buck and headed back to camp. They decided during their hike not to bring up the fact that there was probably more than one Bigfoot to the others. But the idea that more than one was out there scared the hell out of them.

When they arrived back at camp, there was an aroma in the air of fresh fish frying. And, man, did it smell good. It was obvious that Todd also had success on his fishing trip. They all ate and relaxed by the fire.

"You know," JT said, "it might be cold enough at night to make ice so we can store some food in the cooler again."

The temperature was beginning to fall. And the cold air was slipping in earlier than it had over the past couple of days.

JT and Todd went to replenish their water supply for the next day and Bo and Jenny set up the equipment in the new supply tent.

Bo stopped for a moment and asked Jenny to sit down so they could talk. Jenny, surprised that Bo looked so serious, did as he asked and began to listen intently to what Bo was saying.

"You know, I want that footage as badly as everyone else, maybe more than anyone else, but we have to be realistic. This could be very dangerous and I don't want anyone to get hurt. Maybe we should pack up and go."

Jenny had a shocked look on her face and was surprised that Bo, of all people, would bring this up. "What happened while you and JT were hunting to change your mind? I mean, just yesterday you were all gung ho and ready to get rich."

"Jenny, listen to me." Bo reached out and held her hand in his and leaned close to her. "Is it worth our lives? While JT and I were out today, we started thinking about the deer we saw. Why were there three deer? You saw the size of the liver we brought back. Why were there three deer? Let me tell you why. There's more than one of those things out there. This isn't worth our lives."

Jenny pulled her hand away and stood up, obviously furious. "If there's more than one out there, then our odds of finding one just went up and if you want to go, then go. I'm not stopping you. I've waited my whole life for a chance like this and I'm not going to blow it."

Bo stood and gently grabbed her by the arms and puller her closer to him. "Look, I'm not saying give up; I'm just saying maybe we should get the right people and try again."

"No way," she said as she pulled away from his grasp.

"Okay, okay. We'll give it a few more days and if we find ourselves in any real danger, we leave. Agreed?"

"I'm not agreeing to anything," she snapped. "I'll just say we'll take it one day at a time."

It was then that Todd and JT arrived back to camp from their hike for water. They could both sense that they may have arrived at a bad time. Bo, by now, was more determined than ever to get the footage and get the hell out of there, as quickly as possible.

"If we're going to do this, then let's do it right," Bo said with authority.

The others listened as Bo laid out his plan. "First, we need to move the cameras to a better location. I think by the creek bed is the best place, because that seems to be his way in and out of camp. We should also cut the liver up and leave several portions throughout the woods to attract him from different directions and put a large piece by the creek bed. We also need to start sleeping in shifts so we always have someone wide awake watching for it."

The group agreed to the plan and started setting the trap.

By the time everything was set up to Bo's specifications, it was already mid afternoon and it seemed that all they could do was wait.

In the sky, the clouds began to change from the usually fluffy white to dark and gray. The wind started to pick up and the group knew a storm was moving in.

The sound of the coming rain could be heard like a locomotive racing down the tracks. The group didn't even have time to make it to their tents when the rain hit. The rain was falling fast and hard in what seemed like buckets of water just falling from the heavens.

Bo unzipped his tent about two inches, looked out and realized, what was daylight moments ago, seemed to instantly turn to night. The lightning would brighten up the camp like the sunlight, if only for a second at a time, when it flickered in the dark sky. Bo could see the other tents as they were luminated by the lanterns inside.

Then suddenly he saw a figure in the tree line, but only a glimpse. He frantically searched the tree line while waiting for another bolt of lightning to show it again. When the lightning did strike again, he got his wish. In the mere second of light, he got a detailed look at the creature that stood merely yards from the tent occupied by Jenny and Todd.

The horror that struck his gut was almost unbearable. He continued to watch, waiting for another flash of light to see what the creature was doing next. When the sky luminated the area again, the creature was standing right over Jenny's tent. He knew he had to do something, and now.

J.E. BROWN

Bo, without thinking, franticly unzipped his tent and ran out into the rain. Bo was yelling at the top of his lungs, "Get out of here. God damn it, get out of here."

He could see better now that he was outside tent and noticed the look on the creature's face. The look was one of surprise and it seemed to be just as frightened as Bo. He turned to Bo and let out a growling noise that even the others heard through the pounding rain.

Jenny unzipped her tent and began to scream when she noticed that right there in front of her tent was the elusive creature she was looking for.

The creature seemed as terrified as they did. It turned and ran into the tree line with its arms swinging low to the ground and its back hunched over. It didn't take the time to look back at what had scared it away, and in just a few seconds, it was gone. Bo dropped to his knees as his racing heart began to slow to a normal rate.

Jenny ran to Bo and wrapped her arms around his head to make sure he was okay. By now, all four were out of their tents and in the rain. They searched through the darkness, but nothing could be seen.

The rain lasted for an hour longer and darkness began to fade to the late afternoon sunlight that was rightfully supposed to be there.

They checked the monitors and found nothing. This time the creature entered and exited through the trees just yards from the tents. The creature still managed to avoid being seen on film.

"Do you think he knows the cameras are there?" Todd asked, as if to find some logical explanation as to why they'd had multiple encounters and still no credible footage of the beast.

Bo answered, "I doubt it. I think it's just been lucky."

Jenny, who was still visibly shaken from their encounter, sat quietly by the new fire that JT made to warm them up.

The once muddy creek bed was now a running creek and a good source of water, so JT went down to refill the flasks. Upon returning, he informed Bo that the liver they set out to attract the beast was still there.

Now wet, cold, and hungry, Bo decided to carve out some meat from the deer they killed earlier and start making dinner. By the time dinner was over and everyone had dried out, it was starting to turn dark for the second time today.

Bo stood and told the group that he would sit up tonight with camera in hand and watch for the Bigfoot, and everyone else should get a good night's sleep because they didn't know what tomorrow had in store for them.

The group agreed and Jenny, Todd and JT all retired to their tents early in hopes for a quiet night and some much needed rest. The night air was cold and Bo sat by the fire with a blanket draped over his shoulders to help keep him warm. Thoughts of today's encounter went through his head. The monster he had seen was a giant of a man or a beast; he was not quite sure which, but a giant nonetheless. He could remember the confused look on the creature's face. What did it want from them? Was it just curious or did it come into their camp for a reason? How many were there? And was there more than one here today?

The questions ran through his head with enough fury

that Bo now had a headache and the closest drugstore was three hundred miles away.

Suddenly, and without warning, a pine cone smashed into the fire, causing sparks to shoot out from the flame as though a tiny explosion had gone off right in front of him. Bo fell backwards off the log he was using for a chair. He jumped to his feet and began to film as objects periodically flew in from the darkness. After a few minutes, the attack was over and Bo resumed his post on the log.

He watched the incident that he filmed over and over, and then he noticed that the pine cones were coming from different angles, so there must have been more than one out there.

At around two a.m. Bo heard the zipper on Jenny's tent slowly slide down the front of the tent and Jenny crawled out and walked over and sat next to him.

"How's it going?" she asked.

"I'll show you," he responded, and he showed her the film he had been watching for the past hour or so.

"This just happened?"

"Yep, a little while ago. Did you notice that they were thrown from different locations?"

"How many do you think there are?" She was hoping for an answer with a low number.

"My guess is there are three. You know," he said with a smile, "this makes two nights in a row you've come out here to sit with me."

She smiled back and said, "Who said I came out here to sit with you? Maybe I just wanted to make sure you were okay after what happened earlier."

The two talked for a few more minutes when Bo moved closer to Jenny and offered part of his blanket to help keep her warm. Jenny accepted with a smile and moved in even closer.

"You're warm," she said as her eyelids slowly fell shut. She went fast asleep in Bo's arms.

He was happy to know she felt safe where she slept, but wondered why the creature chose her tent. Maybe it was just a coincidence. If it did know she was there, then what was it about to do? Maybe if he had only waited to see… But if he had, it could have been too late. All he knew was she was safe right now. And that's all he cared about.

Chapter 4

Monday, October 16, 2006
Day 4

It was earlier than usual when JT woke up. And he was surprised to find Bo sitting on the ground with his back against a log and Jenny stretched out, still asleep, with her head resting on Bo's lap.

"She looks comfortable," JT joked.

Bo looked down at her and simply replied, "She does, doesn't she?"

Bo handed the camcorder to JT and asked him to watch what happened last night. JT picked up on what Bo wanted him to see right away.

"Holy cow, there is more than one out there."

"Yeah," Bo said, "and here's the thing. I know Jenny isn't going to leave and I'm not leaving without her. But there are things we need out here just to survive. We need someone to go back to the Jeep and drive into town and get a few things and come back. And I don't think anyone should go alone."

JT cut him off and said, "Do you think Todd will be okay leaving his sister out here?"

A voice came in from behind JT saying, "Well, it looks like she's in good hands here."

Bo smiled and assured Todd that she was.

Bo woke Jenny by gently shaking her arm. She looked a little embarrassed waking up with everyone sitting around the now fizzled-out fire.

Bo informed her of the plan and she agreed that it would be best to have new supplies.

"Look, we need food to cook and some things we can eat without cooking, like maybe peanut butter and some bread. We're also going to need a two-way radio so if anything happens, we can call for help. You can't say anything to anybody about what's going on up here. If anyone knew, they would either laugh at you or follow you back—and we don't want either to happen."

Bo also suggested taking a few of the dead batteries back with them to charge in the Jeep while they were gone.

"That's a good idea," JT said. JT and Todd got dressed for their long hike back to the Jeep.

"You guys might want to get a room in town tonight also, so you're not trying to get back to the campsite in the dark," Bo added.

Bo was already figuring if they went straight there and back, it would take about seventeen hours with a five-and-a-half-hour walk to the Jeep and a two-and-a-half-hour drive to town. That would only give them an hour to shop, with the time it would take to get back, and by then it would already be dark.

"Get a room this afternoon and get about six or seven hours of sleep and you should be back about this time in the morning," Bo explained.

The group agreed that this was the best plan. Jenny asked Todd to pick up some warmer clothes for all four of them. The temperature had dropped faster than any of them had imagined.

So JT and Todd got ready to go and they all traded their good-byes and be-carefuls. Then the two men disappeared into the woods.

Jenny already seemed to be worried for Todd and JT. Bo walked over to her and held her close and explained that Todd and JT were now the safest of the four.

Jenny smiled and shook her head in agreement. "I'm sure they'll be fine, but I can't help being afraid for them."

Bo knew he had to come up with something to get her mind off the others, so he suggested an expedition for the two of them.

"You know, we still need to go out there and check on the bait we set out and make sure it's still there. And I was thinking about a little hike ourselves to see if we can learn more about these things."

Jenny was excited to get away from the campsite for a while and Bo was impressed with how brave and calm Jenny had been over the last couple of days. Jenny asked if Bo thought it would be a good idea to set the cameras up in the campsite, just to be sure that if one came while they were gone, they would have it. Bo agreed and the two set out to rearrange the cameras again in the hopes of finishing their quest.

After hiking for about an hour, Todd and JT stumbled onto a campsite that seemed to be vacant. There were two tents set up. Each was facing a cold and damp fire pit. The fire hadn't burned since at least the rain the day before.

With no one here, Todd figured they might be out for a hike, and took it upon himself to rekindle their fire. Even though it was damp, it didn't take any time for him to build a small, warm fire.

The two used the fire to cook the meat they brought with them and ate until their bellies were full. They were cleaning up their mess, when suddenly a large rock came crashing to the ground, missing Todd's foot by just inches. The two men froze and looked into the forest hoping to see where the object came from. It was then that a foul odor overtook the once fresh air they were breathing.

JT looked at Todd and said, "They're probably just trying to scare us off. So, grab your backpack, put it on, and let's just leave."

Todd shook his head okay, and then began to do as JT asked.

The two men went on their way without any more objects being thrown in their direction. However, the smell followed them for the next four hours until they reached Bo's Jeep.

Once in the Jeep, JT explained to Todd that he didn't feel they wanted to hurt anyone, they just didn't want people around them. Todd joked that he didn't want to be around them either, so now they were all happy.

JT started the Jeep and the two drove towards the town of Tionesta, which was the closest town to where they were.

After about a one-and-a-half-hour drive, the two pulled up to a small general store and went inside to see if they had all the items Bo and Jenny asked for. To their surprise, the store carried everything they needed except the two-way radio Bo had asked for. So, JT settled on some long-range walkie-talkies and he grabbed a deck of cards that he hoped would help entertain them.

The store was also loaded with Bigfoot books and souvenirs. JT found one book especially interesting and picked it up as well. The clerk, just making friendly conversation, asked if they were moving into the woods.

They laughed as JT responded, "It sure feels like it." They left the store and began to look for a hotel to get some sleep.

"It sure is going to be nice sleeping in a soft bed," JT said. And Todd agreed. JT could tell that something was bothering Todd and asked if he was okay.

Todd answered, "I'm fine. I just hope Jenny and Bo are."

JT assured Todd that Jenny was in good hands with Bo. "If there was a problem, Bo would make sure that Jenny was taken care of, like last night when he ran out of his tent when he felt you and Jenny might be in danger.

"It's not the first time Bo put his life on the line for some else's safety, you know," JT said to Todd. "Let me tell you a story about Bo when we were in the army. It was four years ago and Bo and I were on a top-secret team of twelve men in Afghanistan trying to locate bin Laden. We were deep in the mountains and the team was fired upon by enemy forces hidden deep in the rocks. We were sitting ducks and probably weren't going to make it much longer as the enemy moved in closer and closer. Two of our men had already taken direct hits and were killed. One of them was our commander on the mission. When Commander Jackson was killed, that left Bo in charge. He ordered us to move into a nearby cave, where he set up a wall of defense, protecting ourselves from our attackers. We took out a couple dozen of the oncoming men as they attacked and we lost one more man in that stand. Bo snuck out through a small opening he found about thirty yards deep in the cave. No one really knows what happened next, and Bo won't talk about it, but every enemy gunman outside the cave was killed, except one. I found myself staring down the nozzle of a Russian assault rifle in the hands of an Afghan soldier. I knew I only had a split second to live, and what goes through your head in only a split second is unreal. Suddenly, the man's head just seemed to explode. Bo shot the man from about forty-five yards away, a direct hit. If it weren't for Bo, I would be dead. We've been best friends ever since. In fact, that's how I got this scar. A bullet grazed a rock right in front of me and I was hit by a piece of rock."

"You're making that up, aren't you?" Todd asked.

"No," JT said. "In fact, because it was a top-secret mission, Bo didn't get the credit he deserved. He was offered the Medal of Honor, but he didn't feel he deserved it just for doing his job. The night his parents were killed in a car crash, they were on their way to watch him receive his medal."

Todd shook his head and the look of his newfound respect for Bo could be seen in his eyes. "Jenny really likes him, you know," Todd said.

"Yeah, I think Bo likes her too," JT responded.

After they arrived at their room and Todd was fast

asleep, JT pulled out the book he bought at the store and began to read it, hoping to learn more about the monster. But he didn't get too far when he too fell asleep.

The day was just getting started for Bo and Jenny as they started out to check on the liver they had used for bait. The liver was placed in locations that weren't going to be easy for Jenny to get to—or so Bo thought. Jenny managed to keep up with Bo stride for stride. They wandered out into the forest and made sure that all the liver was still intact. They found that with the exception of little nibbles from the normal wild life that inhabited the area, all the liver was still there.

As they finished with the last of the liver locations, Jenny asked in a joking manner, "So what now? Do we need to head back?"

Bo looked out at the view that was still every bit as amazing as the first morning he woke up to it and suggested that maybe they have a little fun.

Jenny raised her eyebrows and with a smile asked, "What did you have in mind?"

Bo smiled back and suggested a nature walk without looking for the Bigfoot clues that had seemed to engulf their every thought since the moment they met. Jenny agreed and off they went.

The walk was nice, but the temperature steadily dropped as the day went on. Now cold and tired, they decided to take a break. Finding a spot where they could look out at the mountain range, they sat down and relaxed.

Bo said, without really thinking, "You're quite a woman, aren't you?"

Jenny, embarrassed by the comment, asked, "What do you mean?"

"I've never known a woman who could do the things you do and with such passion. You seem to be loving every second of every minute out here."

"Well," she corrected him, "I didn't love it last night when that thing was standing right outside my tent."

"Yeah, but look at you now," he interrupted. "Here you are still out here and having a great time. I hope that when we get out of here, we can keep in touch."

Jenny moved closer to Bo and pressed her lips against his. The two embraced for a while, and then Jenny gently pulled away and said, "I'm counting on it."

The two smiled and break time was over when an arrow came smashing into a tree, just inches from Bo's head. Bo leaped into the air and grabbed Jenny, pulling her to the ground.

"What the hell was that?" Jenny screamed. The terror in her voice was echoing in Bo's mind.

"Don't tell me those things can shoot arrows now," Bo asked.

Suddenly, a voice came from the tree line that Bo figured was about twenty yards away.

"You like trying to scare people, do ya?" the voice rang out.

Bo frantically searched for an escape route, but quickly realized they were pinned. Another arrow came flying in and pierced itself deep into a tree just above where they were.

"What the hell is your problem?" Bo screamed back at the voice.

The angry voice continued, "Let's see how you like being scared." And another arrow smashed into the trees just above their heads.

"You stay right here and keep your head down," Bo told Jenny.

"No, you can't go out there until we know who we're dealing with."

Bo looked at Jenny and said, "I may not know who he is, but I know where he is." And Bo crawled away into the brush.

The man's voice cried out again. "Come on, show yourself and give me a good shot." And again, another arrow hit into the tree.

Bo crawled on his belly for thirty yards and then slowly lifted his head to find the source of the voice. Then he spotted a man down on one knee and hiding behind a tree, still looking in the direction of Jenny.

He knew he had to do something fast. The man hadn't seen that Bo had escaped their hiding spot yet, so Bo was able to flank the man and began to sneak up on him from behind. The man was taunting Jenny and begging her to show her head, if only for a second. He insisted that that was all he needed, just a second.

Bo finally was just a few feet from the man when he ran at him. The man turned; surprised that Bo made it out without him knowing. Bo smashed into the man with all his might. The man bounced off the tree he was shielding himself behind just moments earlier, but was hit with a sharp right hand that landed on his jaw, knocking him completely unconscious before he even hit the ground.

Bo quickly screamed to Jenny to make sure she was still okay.

Jenny slowly got up and yelled back to Bo, "Are you okay?" She was relieved to see Bo step out from behind the tree the man was shooting at them from.

She ran as fast as she could and leaped into Bo's arms. "Are you okay?" she frantically asked.

"I'm fine," he said, assuring her that he was okay.

Jenny wrapped her arms around him. "I was so worried about you."

Bo calmed her down and said, "We need to tie this guy up before he wakes."

With no rope or string with them, Bo cut the strings off the bow and tied the man's hands behind his back. He also tied the man's feet together; far enough apart that he could walk, but close enough that he wouldn't be able to run. Bo threw the small Irish man over his shoulder and he and Jenny began to walk back to camp.

When they arrived, Bo tied him up tight to a tree at the edge of camp. Then he threw some cold water in the man's face to wake him up. The man slowly came to as he looked around dazed and confused. "What the hell happened?" he asked, with an obvious Irish accent.

Bo stood over the man with the empty bowl in his hand that he had used to throw the water in the man's face.

"You tell me," Bo demanded. "You're the one who decided to start shooting arrows at us." Bo's voice was rough and loud and the man felt intimated.

"Look, you guys were trying to scare me last night, so I was just trying to scare you back."

Bo looked at the man and realized that he was scared to death. "We didn't try to scare you last night," Bo, who was right in the man's face, said to him.

"I've been out here all day and you're the only one out here that I could find."

Bo said to the man, "If we were the ones who tried to scare you, is that any reason to try to kill somebody?" The man looked at Bo and said, "If I was trying to kill you, I wouldn't have missed with that first shot."

Bo stood up and told the man he would untie him in a little while after he and Bo calmed down a little.

Bo walked over to where Jenny was sitting and asker her, "What do you think? Should I let him loose?"

Jenny believed the man really thought that they tried to scare him, but felt that he was trying to kill them. Bo smiled at Jenny and suggested that they could leave him tied up tonight and maybe he'd get a look at what really tried to scare him. Bo untied the man from the tree and moved him by the fire, where he could stay warm. They fed the man and made him as comfortable as possible, being tied up and all.

Bo asked the man his name and the man told him Donald.

"Well, Donald, listen to this." Bo and Jenny spent the next few minutes telling Donald what had happened with them over the past four days. Donald laughed at their story and didn't believe a word of it.

"If I cut you loose, are you going to try anything stupid?" Bo asked.

"Nah, you two seem okay to me now and I don't believe you had anything to do with it, but I still don't believe it was a monster either," he insisted.

Bo pulled out his knife and cut Donald loose. Donald was grateful to be loose and rubbed his wrists that were sore from the bow string Bo had used to tie him up.

"Look," Donald said, "you seem like good kids and, Bo, you have one hell of a right, but, if you guys really believe something is out here, why are you still here? I don't think your right hook will have as much effect on the Bigfoot as it did me."

Jenny laughed at the thought of Bo punching a Bigfoot in the mouth, but knew he was right.

Jenny explained the thrill involved and how they could be the first to ever get undeniable evidence that the creature did exist. Donald wished them good luck, thanked them for dinner, and apologized for shooting arrows at them, as he started to head back to his camp.

Donald stopped and turned to them and asked with a confused look on his face, "Can a Bigfoot build a fire? I went down to the stream this morning to catch some fish and when I got back, someone had built me a pretty good fire."

Bo and Jenny looked at each other, and realized that it had to have been JT and Todd. "No," Jenny said, "Bigfoot can't, but I bet our friends did. Was it around seven or eight this morning?"

"Yeah," he answered, surprised they knew the time.

"There are two more in our party. They went to town for some supplies we needed and they must have stumbled onto your campsite. They will be returning in the morning, so if you see two men coming, don't shoot them!"

Donald laughed and asked, "How could I? You cut the strings off my bow."

The three said goodnight and Donald wandered off into the woods.

There was still about an hour of daylight left and they

decided that if that thing came back tonight, they were going to sleep right through it.

"There's only one problem," Jenny said to Bo with a smile.

"Yeah, and what's that?"

"I can't sleep alone. I need my hero with me."

The two slept all night holding each other tight and keeping each other warm. And as far as they knew, there were no visitors in the night.

Chapter 5

Tuesday, October 17, 2006
Day 5

JT and Todd woke up at three a.m. They showered and headed back to Modoc National Forest, where Bo and Jenny would be waiting. They didn't talk much on the drive back and it was still dark when they parked the Jeep in its familiar spot. They had already packed their backpacks with the new supplies they had gone after and were now ready to make the hike back, as soon as they had a little light to see the way.

"What's the odds that thing is still where it was yesterday?" Todd broke the silence.

JT looked over at Todd and assured him that they were going to be just fine. It wasn't long until the sun broke the plain of the mountains and there was enough light to get started.

Todd was in a hurry to check on his sister and JT had to slow him down several times to lessen the odds of a fall.

"That's all I would need," JT said, "is to carry you, your pack, and my pack."

They walked on for several more hours and were happy not to smell that terrible stench that was always left behind when the creature was close by.

They soon arrived back at the campsite they stopped at the day before when they built the fire. This time it was different! The two tents were collapsed and ripped into pieces. The campfire had been destroyed and there were rocks lying all over the place.

JT made the gruesome discovery of an older red-haired man lying lifeless around the base of a nearby tree. JT raced over to him to see if the man was still alive. He wasn't. He had probably been killed in the middle of the night, because he was frozen almost solid. This was the first time Todd had ever seen a dead body except for a funeral.

"What do you think happened here?" Todd asked.

JT figured he was thrown against the tree by what he guessed was one of the Bigfoot things. But why, he wondered. They weren't violent in any of their encounters. Annoying, he thought, but not violent.

JT told Todd not to touch anything and get back to the campsite and let Bo and Jenny know what they found. Todd agreed and the two men went on their way.

Jenny woke up first this morning and was careful not to wake Bo. She knew he hadn't slept in two days when he fell asleep last night. She stepped out of Bo's tent and went straight to the monitors and watched the tapes to see if they had any visitors last night and was surprised to find they hadn't. She started to wonder if maybe they had moved on after realizing they couldn't scare them off. She thought that maybe her dream of getting one on film may have to wait until another time.

It wasn't long before Bo got up as well. The two sat by the fire to keep warm and waited for JT and Todd to return with some food. This day was starting out colder than the others and the creek that ran past the camp was covered with a layer of ice on the top.

Jenny decided to take out her still-frame camera and finally take some pictures of the view they were able to enjoy every morning. She took a few shots with Bo hamming it up and then Bo took some with her in them.

"These are going to be great," she announced.

Bo loved to watch her when she was so happy. He couldn't believe he was falling for a girl he had only known for a few days, but they had been through more in the past few days than most people went through in years.

The two found themselves in each other's arms again sitting by the fire. She could feel his muscles through his shirt as she rubbed his arm, and felt as though she belonged there. She could tell that Bo felt the same way by the way he held her as though nothing was ever going to take her away. She liked the fact that she felt safe and secure there and she didn't want the feeling to end.

JT and Todd arrived, making their way through the woods. Jenny ran to her brother and gave him a hug. She was so glad that they were back and okay. She then turned and hugged JT also and thanked him for making sure Todd was okay. Bo had reached them by now and he reached out to shake his buddy's hand. JT looked at Bo and motioned with his head that they needed to talk in private. JT and Todd agreed not to upset Jenny if they didn't have to.

Todd and Jenny walked over to the fire and sat down to warm up, and Bo and JT walked down by the creek to talk.

"What's up? Bo asked.

"We found a body in a campsite about an hour away from here. I think the Bigfoot killed him."

Right away Bo remembered Donald had walked in that direction and he also mentioned someone starting a fire at his campsite.

"Was it the same campsite you made a fire on your way out yesterday?"

JT was surprised by the question. "I didn't say anything about a fire on our way out yesterday. How did you know about that?"

"Donald mentioned it to us," Bo answered.

"Donald, who's Donald?"

"He's the guy who tried to kill Jenny and me yesterday."

JT, even more confused than before, asked, "What the hell happened while we were gone?"

"Come on," Bo said. "I'll explain everything to ya."

And he started walking towards the fire. JT followed closely behind. When they reached the fire, they sat down and Bo and Jenny began telling JT and Todd about how they met Donald and let him go.

"I would have killed the psycho," Todd muttered.

Bo looked at Todd, understanding what he was saying, and replied, "Looks like someone or something did that for us."

Jenny, surprised by the comment, looked at Bo and he looked at her.

"JT just told me they found a body about an hour back. He said it looks like the work of one of our friends."

Jenny was stunned by the news and had the same thought that JT did when they found the body.

"Let's eat first," Bo said, "and then JT and I will walk back and bury him in a place where we can find him later."

During breakfast, Jenny mentioned the fact that this must explain why the monster or monsters didn't show up here last night.

"But why did they kill him and not us?" she asked.

Bo, who had already pondered the same question, was quick to answer. "He was the type to attack before even knowing what was out there. He must have heard something or they were throwing things at his campsite and he just went in half cocked."

JT affirmed Bo's suspicions by mentioning that there were rocks lying all over the campsite, much like the pine cones here just a few nights ago.

When they were done with their breakfast, Bo and JT grabbed their crossbows and headed towards Donald's campsite. They didn't talk much on the way; instead they listened to the sounds of the forest for any noises that didn't belong.

As they approached the campsite, they heard growling and rustling coming from the site. Bo and JT ducked into some brush and quietly snuck up on what was making the noise. What they found were five wolves fighting over the dead body of Donald. Both men took aim and fired shots deep into two of the wolves. The others, surprised by the attack, ran into the trees.

Bo and JT walked to where the mangled body of Donald lay sprawled out and ripped to shreds. The left arm of the carcass was torn almost completely off the body.

Bo, who had seen many dead bodies in the past, was visibly shaken up by what he was looking at.

JT quickly picked up some material that was once one of the tents and laid it over the body. Bo asked if all the damage to the body was already there or was that the work of the wolves. JT explained that when they found him, he was lying at the bottom of a tree that was only several feet from where the body lay now. JT explained that the only injury to the body when they first found it was a broken neck and a broken back. There was also some bruising on the left side of his face.

"I would think that the bruising was my doing," Bo explained.

JT reached into his pack and pulled out a shovel. "Where do you want to do this?" he asked.

Bo looked around and noticed a clearing about fifteen yards from where they stood and the men began to dig.

Back at camp, Todd was telling Jenny what JT told him about the Afghanistan story. Jenny listened intently as Todd retold the story, but with more excitement. When Todd told her of the part about Bo's parents, a tear slowly rolled down her cheek.

She told Todd about their encounter with Donald and how Bo snuck around him and took him out to save her life.

"The two stories are a lot alike," she said.

When Bo and JT finished their chore, the two men decided to look around and see if, one, there was any evidence that Bigfoot had killed Donald, and, two, see if Donald had anything that they could take back to their camp. They didn't find anything except the rocks that lay scattering the campsite floor that proved the Bigfoot had been there, but they both suspected that it had been.

During their search for any items they could take back with them for their own use, they found some cooking utensils and a little food. They also found that Donald had already replaced the strings on his bow, but the best thing they found was a map of the area that had several caves circled and had very detailed terrain elevations. They took what they could carry, including the bow and around thirty or so arrows, the map, and headed back to their camp.

When they arrived back at their campsite, they told Jenny and Todd about the wolves; the shape the body was in made it impossible to determine that a Bigfoot had killed him. This fact was only important to proving that the beast existed, they already knew without any doubt the Bigfoot killed him.

JT went to his tent and retrieved the book he bought at the general store that he and Todd visited and began to explain some of what he had read.

He told them about the discovery of three jawbones and a bunch of teeth they had found of a bipedal ape-like creature the science community named Gigantopithecus. He showed the picture of a model the scientists made to show what they felt the creature looked like.

"My God," Bo exclaimed. "That looks just like what I saw in the rain the other night."

Jenny started to shake when she viewed the picture. At this point, she had gotten the closest look at the monster as it stood just three feet from her when she opened her tent the day it rained. Bo moved closer to her and put his arm around her and pulled her tight. She felt that now familiar sense of security that she had grown to love.

JT could see that the two of them should be alone for a while to soak up what they just saw in the book.

He looked over at Todd and asked if he knew how to shoot a bow. Todd was excited about the idea of doing some target practice and having some fun, something that seemed to have eluded the group to this point.

The two stood up and went down to the creek, where JT carved out a target on a large tree trunk. JT showed Todd how to hold the bow and aim and how important the release was to a good shot.

Todd picked it up quickly and was soon hitting the target on almost every shot. While Todd practiced, JT walked back up to the campsite and sat down by the fire. He looked up into the sky and told Bo and Jenny that while in their hotel room, the weatherman on television said that they could be getting some snow tonight or tomorrow.

Bo and Jenny began to look up as well. The sun was out, but the air was still cold. "I hope this is one of those times he's wrong," Bo said with a hint of laughter.

JT, who remembered the map at that point, asked if Bo had looked it over yet.

"I almost forgot about the map," Bo answered, and he stood up to retrieve it from his back pocket. Bo laid the map out and began to point out several locations on it.

"We are right about here," he said, "and this is where Donald set up camp. This is where we found the dead deer."

And then, while he was pointing to the spot he and Jenny were at when Donald began shooting arrows at them, he noticed how close they had been to a cave that was circled with a red marker.

"He wasn't camping," Bo exclaimed. "He was looking for these caves. That's why they killed him, he found where they live!"

Bo had never seemed so sure of himself. Jenny, on the other hand, wasn't convinced.

"Why didn't they kill him there?" she asked. "I mean, if he found where they live, wouldn't they have killed him there? Why wait until he got back to his camp?"

Bo knew it was a good question, and didn't have an answer yet.

So, he just said, "Maybe he took something from them and they went to get it back."

"He didn't have anything with him when he was here," she said. "And he was killed that night."

Again, Jenny made a good point and Bo didn't have an answer for it, but he could feel in his gut that he was right.

"What happened?" he asked himself. He scanned Donald's campsite in his mind. "The tents!" he said. "Didn't it look like they may have been looking for something?"

JT reminded Bo about how his tent had been pulled up and thrown all the way to the creek.

"Damn it!" Bo shouted under his breath. "I'm missing something."

JT stood up and joked, saying he had to go check on Robin Hood, and walked back down to the creek.

"Bo," Jenny said, "it's okay, we'll figure it out."

Bo looked at Jenny and said, "I'm telling you, these things live in one of these caves. I don't think he was out here looking for these things," Bo added, "but he found them. I just wonder what it was he was looking for."

Bo looked at Jenny and told her that he had to go back to Donald's campsite and look around some more.

"JT said that you guys searched the campsite," she responded. "And that this stuff was all you found. You didn't find any footprints or anything that would suggest that Bigfoot had been there except the rocks on the ground."

"I'm not going to be looking for evidence that Bigfoot was there, I'm going to be looking for notes or something to tell us why Donald was out here."

"Well," she said, "it's going to take a few hours to do that and it's going to be dark soon, so wait until tomorrow and we'll all go and help you search."

Bo knew she was right, there were only a couple of hours of light left and this would be the best way to keep her safe. So, he agreed, and the two of them walked down to the creek to check on the progress Todd had made with his newly found hobby. Jenny clapped and gave Todd encouragement every time he hit the target, which by now was much more frequent.

Todd was starting to look at JT as more of the big brother that was missing in his life than one of the guys they just happened to meet in the woods. In fact, the entire group was closer now, and they felt more like a family than just friends.

Jenny watched as Bo and JT took Todd under their wing and it made her feel proud of Todd as he learned the skills taught by the two men. After a few minutes of watching, Bo waved Jenny over and let her take a few shots at the target. All the arrows that reached the tree sailed past to the left or right. Most just skipped up and stopped short.

As darkness fell, they moved back to their spots by the fire. Todd asked Bo to tell his story of Afghanistan, hoping he would tell what happened outside the cave.

Bo looked at JT and JT looked away, knowing he wasn't supposed to tell the story. Bo looked back and Todd and just said that what happened out there four years ago was a horrible thing.

He continued saying, "What I did, I had to do to save the lives of the men that served with me. I only did what had to be done. If JT had been in charge that day, he would have done the same thing. I'm no hero; I'm no better than anyone else. I was put in a position I didn't want to be in."

Bo stood up and politely said good night and walked to his tent and climbed inside. Todd felt bad for bringing it up, but JT explained that he should have told Todd not to mention it and took the blame upon himself.

Jenny excused herself and walked over to Bo's tent and asked if she could come in. Bo held her hand with his and apologized for waking away the way he had. Jenny explained that it was okay to be a hero and after what happened the day before, it didn't matter what had happened in Afghanistan, he would always be a hero to her.

Bo smiled and rolled over to face her and held her tight.

"I guess it's not bad to be your hero," he said. She smiled back at his comment. Bo said, with a disappointed look on his face, "I guess I should go out there and apologize to Todd for walking away."

Jenny answered, "He understands."

Outside the tent, Todd and JT were planning a hunt for the next days so Todd could try out his new talent on something other than a tree.

Suddenly, the terrible smell they associated with the Bigfoot filled the air and JT yelled to Bo to come out.

Bo and Jenny hurried out of the tent and were hit with the stench right away. Bo quickly determined the monster must be to the west because the wind was blowing from the west, and had picked up over the past few minutes. This made it hard to tell how close the beast was. Todd suddenly jumped to his feet and pointed to the tree line, too scared to say anything. They all looked in that directions and saw, without a doubt, the beast standing in the tree line only eighty yards or so from where they were.

It stood there for several seconds, just looking back at them, and then it began to make a howling noise that seemed to echo throughout the wilderness. Then they heard knocking noises coming from different directions. They seemed to be surrounded by whatever was making those noises. The creature seemed to be warning them that there was more than one and they had better leave. Jenny grabbed her handheld camera and began to film what they were watching. She finally had what she came to get—Bigfoot on tape!

The monster stood there for several more seconds before turning and disappearing into the woods. The sounds in the forest continued for a while before they stopped.

The entire group was excited by the fact that they had it; they had the proof they needed and could finally get the hell out of this place.

But when they watched what Jenny had filmed, they noticed that the shadows of the trees covered on tape what they could so clearly see with their own eyes. The beast had yet again managed to avoid what would certainly be proof that it existed.

"I can't believe this," Jenny said. "I had it. It was right here."

Bo put his arm around her waist and assured her that they would get it. The night fell fast and it began to get even colder. The group decided to get some sleep and decide the next course of action in the morning. They all went to bed and fell fast asleep.

Chapter 6

Wednesday, October 18, 2006
Day 6

The night was cold and, like predicted, snow had covered the campsite in the night. Todd was the first one awake and decided he would get the fire started so they could all stay warm when they awoke. After he started the fire, he began to make breakfast. The smell of bacon filled the air and soon the others would be enjoying the warm fire and eating breakfast. It didn't take long. Jenny was the next one up, followed by JT. Bo slept a little longer, but he was up in time to eat a hot meal.

The snow was wet and packed easily, so JT made a snowball and nailed Todd in the back with it as he was getting more wood for the fire. It didn't take long until all four were engaged in a giant snowball fight. There weren't any teams; it was just a free-for-all. It was the most fun they'd had in their five days together.

When the snowball fight was over, they all went back to the fire to dry out their gloves and warm up.

Bo made it a point to apologize to Todd for walking away the night before. Todd said he understood and told Bo that he felt bad for bringing it up again.

"You know," Todd said, "we should build a snowman."

JT smiled and admitted that it did sound like a good idea.

Bo mentioned that he was going back to Donald's campsite to see if he could find anything else. Jenny figured that even though it would be a good idea if they all went, she would let Todd stay with JT so they could build a snowman and enjoy it out here for a change.

She and Bo grabbed their packs and, out of water, they walked down to the creek first to refill their flasks. The creek was frozen over, so Bo threw a big rock on the surface of the ice and made a good-size hole in the top.

They filled their flasks with the cold water that ran beneath the surface. They started to walk away when Bo stopped and turned to look at the hole he had made in the ice.

"That's it," he said.

Jenny, confused, asked, "What's it?"

The hole in the ice reminded Bo of the cave entrances.

"They travel through the caves. I'll bet they live in the caves, and much like a house, they have more than one way in and out. They travel underground, like the water under the ice!" he exclaimed.

Jenny didn't see any reason this couldn't be true, but she didn't understand how it was relevant to what they were doing.

Bo smiled and told Jenny that all they needed to do was find out which cave they used the most and set up a camera there. Bo and Jenny were very excited about the idea, and knew that if they found the right one, it would be easy to set up a camera.

They ran back to the fire and explained their ideas to JT and Todd.

The entire group was happy with the plan, when JT asked, "How do we find out which cave is the one they use?"

"Look," Bo answered, "most of our experiences with these things have happened at night. Not all, but most."

"Right," JT said, not understanding where Bo was going with this.

"If we look during the day for signs at the cave entrance like footprints, broken branches, or whatever we find," Bo said, "then we set up there for a day. If we don't find anything, we move on to the next one. In just a few days, we're bound to catch something on tape."

"*If* they're living in the caves," Jenny added. Not that she disputed what Bo was saying, but to her, it just seemed too easy.

"Why hasn't anyone else done it before?" she asked.

"My bet," Bo said, "is because no one who was looking for these things had a map like this of the caves. Listen, if we find Donald was keeping notes or anything like that at all, we could narrow down the search."

JT asked, "What if the caves he's circled are the ones he already found? He could have been looking for more, and there could be more caves out there that we don't even know about."

Bo agreed with JT and said, "Right now, with the information we have, this is our best shot at getting this thing on film."

The group thought about it for a while and all agreed Bo was right. This was the best plan they had out of all the ones that Bo had come up with.

But was it safe? Todd, who usually didn't ask a lot of questions, asked, "How safe would it be to go right up to their front door and set up a camera? I mean, if they are in there and they hear us or even smell us outside the cave, we're toast."

The group sat quietly for a while when Bo said, "That's why only JT and I can go."

Jenny wasn't happy a bit with what Bo had just said and informed him that she would go whether he liked it or not.

Bo looked over at Jenny and responded, "Look, someone will have to stay here at camp with Todd, and, well, JT and I have training moving about in the woods quietly."

"I thought you said you believe they usually sleep during the day," she snapped back.

Bo was growing irritated about the argument that she kept going on with and finally snapped back, "Look, I'm not going to take the chance of you getting hurt out there. I'm not going to lose you after I just found you. Listen," his voice softened, "I'm falling for you and I just don't want you to get hurt."

Jenny reached over and held Bo's hand and asked, "How am I going to get hurt with my hero with me the whole time?"

Bo realized that it wouldn't do any good to argue with her and admitted that Todd would be more protected with JT here instead of Jenny. And it would be nice to have her with him, so he could keep an eye on her.

Bo looked over at JT and asked, "Well, what do you think?"

"Whatever you think is best," JT answered. "I don't have a problem hanging out with Robin Hood here," as he playfully punched Todd in the arm.

"Okay, then, I guess it's decided. The plan is, Jenny and I will head over to Donald's camp and see what we can find there while you two build your snowman. When we get back, we'll eat lunch and head back out to find the first cave."

During their hike to Donald's campsite, Bo took the opportunity to give Jenny a crash course in how to move quietly through the woods and how to hide if they saw something. Jenny learned the techniques her teacher was explaining to her fast and even surprised Bo with how fast she learned. But Bo knew that this was just a Basic Adventures course 101 and would only help a little, but a little was better than none, he thought.

When they arrived at Donald's camp, Jenny quickly realized something that the others didn't. This was the same spot that she and Todd had camped at their first night.

After a short discussion about that fact, she looked at Bo and said, "It could have been Todd and I that were killed here instead of Donald."

Bo looked at her and said, "Yeah, but it wasn't."

She thought about how lucky she was to have found Bo and JT but kept her thoughts to herself. She didn't want Bo to change his mind about her going with him to the caves.

The two started sifting through the snow to see if they could find anything.

Jenny noticed two lumps in the snow and walked over to investigate. She realized, after kicking one of them around, that they were made by the two wolves that Bo and JT had shot the day before with their crossbows.

As they searched, the snow began to fall again and quickly covered the tracks they made as they entered the campsite. They were just about to give up when Jenny noticed under a piece of material that was once the tent Donald slept in was a metal lock box.

Bo pried the box open with his knife and inside they found exactly what they were looking for.

He reached over and pulled Jenny to him and said, "You're amazing," as he pressed his lips firmly against hers.

She accepted the comment and kissed him back with the same intensity. After a long kiss, they started back to camp.

Meanwhile, back at camp, the snowman was coming along pretty well. They decided to build it in the shape of their nightly visitor, and when they were done, they named it Giganto, which was short for Gigantopithecus; the scientific name for what they believed was out there.

It looked pretty good and was around six feet tall, much shorter than the seven or maybe even eight feet tall they felt the real ones were.

They built it down by the creek so it wouldn't melt by the fire, and there was a larger area there to get the snow. As they finished their project, the snow began to fall. JT walked up to his tent and retrieved the bow they were using the evening before and Todd continued with his practice while JT watched.

The snow that was falling made it hard for Bo and Jenny to return to camp. The terrain was hard to navigate and was now slippery to boot. But even though it took a little longer, they managed to find their way back to camp.

Bo and Jenny wondered where JT and Todd had slipped off to when they heard the familiar sound of arrows hitting a tree. They made their way down to the creek and were surprised by the snowman the other two had built.

JT saw them coming down the hill and asked, "What do you think of Giganto?" Bo just shook his head and Jenny laughed as they checked it out.

"Wow," Jenny said, "this looks great."

Todd went over to Jenny and insisted she watch how good he had gotten with the bow. While she watched Todd, JT walked over to Bo and asked if they found anything.

"Well," he said, "she did. That woman never stops amazing me." Bo paused as he watched Jenny with Todd.

JT patted Bo on the back and said, "So, what did she find?"

"She found a lock box that contained a journal that Donald was keeping. He had only been here for one day, and at his age, there's no way he could have gone to all those caves. The journal mentions that he was considering moving his campsite because he felt there was something close that had died. I'm assuming that he is referring to the smell the Bigfoot makes. He does mention one cave in the journal, but I'm not sure which one it is. He wrote that the opening to the cave is only about five feet in diameter and it's covered by heavy brush." He continued, "And I quote, 'I went into the opening of the cave that is the doorway to a very large room that one must climb down a steep wall to reach the floor. Tomorrow I will bring ropes and try to make the descent to the bottom, which I can only guess is about twenty feet down.'"

Bo stopped reading and explained that to Donald that would have probably been a hard climb, but to them it would be easy, and to Bigfoot it would be nothing.

JT asked, "What else does the journal say?"

"That's it," Bo said. "It was just a one-day journal. But now we know what to look for."

Bo gave JT a high five and the two were obviously happy that they were now one step closer to getting this thing on film.

Jenny shared in their enthusiasm from afar as she watched the men celebrate. Todd seemed oblivious to the excitement going on around him as he continued to put arrow after arrow into the tree.

When Todd had finished and the four of them were about to head back to camp, Jenny noticed that Bo looked at the Giganto, pointed his finger at it, and made the comment, "You're going down, Giganto!"

The group made their way back to the camp. They ate a late lunch and Jenny asked when they were going to head out to find the first cave. Bo pulled out the map and found the one out of the five that was closest to where they were.

"I think this one is the one to hit today."

They gathered up their equipment and put it into their backpacks.

Bo, armed with his crossbow, and Jenny bundled up and, carrying most of the equipment, were just about to leave when JT took Bo aside and told him that it might be a good idea to teach her the hand signals for communicating without making noise.

Bo agreed, but said he would have to do it on the way because if they waited any longer, they might not make it back before dark. So they headed out in the direction of the first cave.

JT and Todd sat around the fire for a while talking about the future. Todd was only nineteen and at the age where most guys think they have crossed the threshold into manhood, but too young to realize they haven't.

"You should be in school," JT told him.

"Yeah, that's what Jenny always tells me," Todd replied. "If I had gone to school this fall, I wouldn't have been able to come out here with her and, let's be honest; I wouldn't have learned as much in school as I have out here. I'm not saying I'm not going to go to school, but it is nice to take some time to enjoy life."

JT understood exactly what Todd was saying because he too had had the same decision to make and he chose the army.

"What about the army?" JT asked. "Has that crossed your mind yet?"

"It has," Todd answered. "But I'm not sure I would fit in there."

"No one does," JT said. "You're molded into that type. It's not something everyone is cut out for. I'm sure whatever you decide will be the right choice."

The two talked on for quite a while.

When Bo and Jenny were about halfway there, they stopped to take a break. Bo told her that according to the map, the terrain was about to get even harder. That's when Jenny noticed the three mounds in the snow that reminded her of the wolves she had discovered back at Donald's camp.

"Look at that." She pointed towards them.

Bo walked over and moved the snow off with his foot and realized that she had just found three more deer lying much the same way as the others they found a few days ago.

"Look at this," he said. "Three again." They all had broken necks and at least one broken leg and one of them had two legs that had been broken. And like before, their stomachs were ripped open and the intestines were pulled partially out of their bellies. They could only assume that their livers were gone, because neither of them wanted to search inside the animals.

Jenny pulled out her camera and took some still photos of their find and the two hiked up the hill.

As they walked, Bo went over some of the hand motions that he would use if they were ever in a situation where they couldn't talk or had to maintain silence.

Jenny picked up on the signals fairly quickly, as Bo expected. And as they walked, Jenny soon realized that Bo was right, the terrain had gotten harder to navigate. They were climbing down into small ravines and then climbing back up the other side. The snow that was still falling wasn't helping. She found hidden logs and hidden rocks under the snow and her feet were beginning to hurt when Bo, who was several feet ahead, ducked quickly behind a small hill and signaled for her to do the same.

She could feel her heart racing. Was Bigfoot just ahead or was he just looking around? She slowly and quietly reached out and tapped Bo's foot. He turned and motioned for her to stay there and keep quiet. He then lifted his head over the hill and surveyed the landscape. She noticed that he didn't seem to be scanning anymore, but just staring in the woods. He slowly ducked back down behind the hill and motioned for her to give him the camera.

She reached down and without thinking unzipped the pocket that held the camera. The sound of the zipper seemed to echo throughout the forest.

Bo quickly motioned for her to stop unzipping the pocket. He dropped his head back in disbelief and slowly made his way back to the crest of the hill without the camera. Jenny could tell that Bo was disappointed and she felt the same about herself. Bo slid back down the hill and motioned for her to turn and quietly sneak away from their location. Jenny turned and did exactly what Bo had asked.

They crawled and moved from hiding spot to hiding spot until they were back to the same place they found the three dead deer.

"What did you see?" Jenny, who was finally able to talk, asked.

"Oh, my God, it was incredible! There were three of those things and they were each digging into a deer, just like these. When I asked for the camera, they had no idea we were even close. They didn't even know we were there. Then, when you unzipped the pocket, I looked again. They didn't see me, but they were all standing and looking in our direction. If you hadn't made so much noise with that damn zipper, we would have had it."

Jenny felt terrible for making the noise and Bo could see the disgust in her eyes.

Bo looked at Jenny and said, "Here's the good news. We can mark this cave off the list because I don't think they would be eating so close to home."

Jenny wished she had been thinking when she unzipped her pocket. "I'm so sorry," she said.

Bo put his arm around her and told her not to worry about it. It was a learning experience.

The two headed back to camp. When they arrived at the camp, they weren't surprised to see Todd practicing with his bow and JT giving tips and advice.

When JT spotted Bo and Jenny, he asked how it went.

And Jenny right away said, "I blew it."

"No, you didn't," Bo said. "You just blew that chance. That's all." He was smiling when he said it and Jenny smiled back.

"Okay," JT asked. "What did she blow?"

"We came up on three of them digging into the bellies of deer. They were so into what they were doing, they didn't even know we were there."

"Great," JT said. "Did you film it?"

"Well," Jenny answered, "that's where I blew it. Bo asked for the camera and when I unzipped my pocket, I wasn't thinking and it made a loud sound. They heard the noise, but didn't see us, so we had to get out of there before they did."

Bo said, "I don't mean to interrupt, but I'm freezing. Can we talk about it by the fire?" Bo told everyone what he had seen and described the three monsters as a family.

"I think," he explained, "there's a mom, dad, and a younger one. If they had seen us, they probably would have killed us because they would have felt that we were there to steel their food. I bet they were at Donald's campsite when he arrived back there the other night. That's probably why they killed him."

"So, what did they look like?" Todd asked.

"Well, it's hard to say," Bo answered. "They were eating and had blood all over their faces. It was kind of scary looking at them when I looked over the ridge to see if they had heard the zipper. By then they were all standing up and facing our direction. The mom, I would guess at about seven feet tall, and the younger one was only about six foot six or so. But the dad, he was a giant. He had to be about eight and a half feet tall. I think it was the mom that was standing over your tent a few nights ago." Bo was looking at Jenny. "Tomorrow we go to a different cave and try to set up the cameras."

Jenny agreed and assured Bo that the mistake wouldn't happen again. Bo smiled and asked who was making dinner. The darkness fell upon the campsite again and the snow stopped falling. And for the second night in a row, the group slept without any visitors.

Chapter 7

Thursday, October 20, 2006
Day 7

Before the light of day had begun to shine, Bo was already up with a fire burning to keep him warm. The sounds of the night seemed to put him at ease while the others slept. He wondered what was going to happen when they left the wilds of the forest.

Would he and Jenny continue on with what he hoped would be a lifelong relationship? He felt that she felt the same as he did, but with him living in Oregon and her in Nevada, would they get the chance to see one another enough to reach the next step?

He knew he would be willing to move there, but would she want him to uproot his life like that? After all, they had only known each other a short time.

These were the thoughts that were going through his head when they were interrupted by a sound he had never heard before, a sound that seemed to come from the creek, just south of where he sat.

Bo jumped to his feet and grabbed the camera that had

infrared night vision and ran to the top of the ridge overlooking the creek.

He started to film the area, but nothing was visible from this distance. He began to make his way down the hill when he heard Jenny call his name. He stopped and went back to the campsite.

Jenny seemed to panic when she realized Bo wasn't in his tent and she didn't see him around the campsite. She was relieved as he approached from out of that darkness that would soon be made luminescent by the sunlight.

"Where were you?" she asked.

Bo could sense that she was worried.

"I'm fine," he said. "I just went over the hill there to see what that noise was."

"What noise?" She looked puzzled as she asked. "I've been in my tent awake for a while and I didn't hear anything."

Bo tried to explain the noise as a sound made by a stack of empty boxes falling from a shelf. She looked even more puzzled now than before.

"I can't explain it," he said. "It was just a noise and I think it came from down there."

Jenny talked him into waiting a few more minutes until they had a little light and they both could go and investigate.

Bo agreed and they went over by the fire and Bo sat on the log while Jenny sat on the ground in front of him. He rubbed her shoulders while the fire crackled and popped.

As the light began to fill the sky, they noticed that most of the snow had melted in the night. The temperature did seem to be a little warmer this morning compared to recent mornings, but it was still cold.

They started walking over the hill and down to the creek when they noticed that Giganto had fallen over. Bo figured that that was probably the sound he heard. With the temperature rising and the snow melting, it seemed to make sense, until they reached the pile of snow that used to be the creation of Todd and JT. What they found were giant handprints, one on each side of the pile. Bo couldn't believe his eyes. It seemed as though the real Giganto attacked or maybe tried to tackle the one made by Todd and JT.

The handprint was there from the beast trying to get to his feet. Bo explained to Jenny what he thought. There were footprints right next to the handprints, which would explain it. But Jenny couldn't imagine why on earth Bigfoot would just run up and tackle the snowman.

"What if in the dark, he thought it was real and he thought there was another Bigfoot in their territory?" he surmised.

"Well, it's better than anything I could come up with," she said with a laugh. Then she noticed something dark in the pile of snow. She was surprised to find that their friend had left some hair behind.

She was excited about finding some hair samples and quickly ran to the campsite to retrieve a baggy so she could collect it.

As they walked back to the campsite, Jenny looked at Bo and said with a smile, "Boxes, huh?"

Bo laughed. "It's all I could think of to explain it."

Todd and JT were up and they were all sitting around the fire enjoying breakfast. Bo was telling JT and Todd about what he guessed had happened to their Bigfoot snowman and they laughed about what the creature's face must have looked like when it realized it wasn't real.

Jenny sat listening quietly as she thought about how they had come so far that now they were making jokes about the monsters. It wasn't long ago she herself was screaming at the sight of one of the beasts standing outside her tent. This wasn't to say she wouldn't scream again in the same situation, but it was funny how the experiences they had now didn't seem to affect them as they used to. She remembered how paranoid they became when they discovered footprints in the mud and how they often wondered if they were being watched.

She just hoped that they hadn't become too relaxed about the situation they were in and let their guard down. The days they had shared had been long and mentally demanding. She knew that at any second one of the beasts could come out of nowhere and attack them without warning.

Would they be ready, she wondered. Bo could tell that Jenny hadn't heard anything that was said over the past few minutes, and he asked her if she was okay. Jenny just smiled and said she was fine. He accepted her answer and they continued on with their conversation.

JT started picking up all the dirty dishes and asked Todd to walk with him to the creek to rinse them off. Todd agreed and the two made their way to the creek.

"You sure you're okay?" Bo asked Jenny again.

"Yeah," she said, "I was just thinking about how laid back we've all gotten. We have to be alert and ready for anything. These things have already killed one man that we know of and they're dangerous."

Bo reached over and pulled Jenny close. He assured her that she and Todd were both in good hands and they were always ready for anything.

Jenny knew that Bo was right and she was probably just overanalyzing, so she broke off the conversation by asking Bo which cave they were going to look for that day.

Bo pulled the map out of his pocket and looked it over.

"I think this one," he said, as he pointed at one of the circles drawn on the map. "The terrain will be a little better."

That was important because of the amount of mud they had now after most of the snow had melted.

He showed her that the only bad spot should be about four miles from the cave, where there seemed to be a large stream or river.

"It will take us several hours to hike to the cave as long as we don't have a problem getting across the stream."

JT and Todd walked up from the creek with clean dishes in hand. Bo informed JT of Jenny's concerns and reminded him to stay alert.

JT assured Bo and Jenny that he was completely aware of the situation the camp was in and he wouldn't let them down. Bo and Jenny knew JT was ready for whatever may happen, but worried more for Todd.

Bo and Jenny picked up their gear and got ready for their hike to the unknown region where the cave was and headed out.

After they were gone, JT went over the situation again with Todd. He could tell Todd understood and they grabbed the bow that Todd had now claimed as his and went out for a little target practice.

After a couple of hours hiking through thick brush and going up and down over a few hills, Bo and Jenny came up on the stream they had seen on the map. It was too cold to try to just walk through it and they weren't sure how deep it was either. Bo looked around to see if he could find any other way over the water, but didn't see an easy answer.

He looked over the map again and decided that their best chance was to walk about a mile upstream to what they hoped was a narrower part of the stream, but with all the water that was running down the stream from the snow that had melted and the rain they had a few days ago, he really didn't think it would be much easier.

When they arrived at the spot they were looking for, they found there was a narrow spot with several large rocks they could jump across, but he knew it would be dangerous with the current being swifter here because of the stream being shallower in this location and combined with the fact that the stream was also narrower.

Bo told Jenny he was going to go first and that she should watch every rock he hit so she could follow on the same path. Bo jumped from rock to rock until he had made it to solid ground again.

Then Jenny followed, hitting every rock that Bo had landed on. She was almost to the end when she slipped and fell. She managed to grab the rock so she wasn't taken downstream in the current, but her body from the chest down was now submerged in the rapid flow of the stream.

Bo quickly dropped all the bags he was carrying and began to make his way to her. He reached down and grabbed her hand and started pulling her back on top of the rock. Once there, the two sat for a moment until Jenny was ready to continue across.

Bo started a fire while Jenny stripped down and wrapped a blanket around her body. She sat close to the fire shivering as Bo held her close.

"I thought I lost you there," Bo said, while kissing her on the forehead.

Jenny cried as she thought about what may have happened if she were unable to grab the rock.

Bo softly reminded her that she was fine and everything was okay. As soon as her clothes dried and she was dressed again, the two ventured on towards the cave.

Todd and JT were having quite the adventure themselves.

The two had wandered out about a mile and a half from the campsite when JT noticed a family of deer that had stopped for a drink in the creek.

JT looked at Todd and pointed down to the deer. Todd raised his bow and took aim at a doe that had raised its head and looked in their direction. As Todd released the arrow, the doe spun and ran into the trees and out of sight. The others followed the lead of the doe and in just a second, they all were gone.

The arrow skipped across the ground and came to rest at the bottom of the creek. Todd was disappointed that he missed and was surprised to see how excited JT was.

"That was so close. Next time, you got it."

Todd frowned and the look of failure was written all

over his face. JT explained that the shot he took was a difficult shot because he had to shoot through the heavy growth of vegetation that separated him from the deer.

"You've only been shooting for a couple of days and almost pulled off a shot like that." JT was proud of the progress made by Todd, but Todd still thought he should have had it. They headed back to camp empty handed.

When Bo and Jenny were only about half a mile from the cave, Bo told Jenny it was time to communicate with hand signals again. They made their way slowly to an area overlooking the cave entrance.

It wasn't the one Donald mentioned in his journal but looked like one that could easily be used by the Bigfoot. It was larger than the one Donald wrote about, but was still well hidden by thick brush.

Bo signaled to Jenny to stay here and he ventured in for a closer look. Careful not to make noise, Bo made his way to only yards from the cave, when he noticed a broken branch about five feet high and at least two inches thick.

He turned to Jenny, who could still see him, and gave her thumbs up and then waved for her to follow.

Jenny was determined not to mess it up this time as she slowly and quietly made her way to Bo.

He leaned over to her and softly whispered that he was going to check out the cave entrance and she was not to move until he signaled for her. She nodded and Bo made his way to the cave.

The entrance was about eight feet high and about fifteen feet wide. He didn't smell what he expected to if the monster had been there, so he climbed into the hole.

Jenny could feel her heart beating fast as she worried about Bo being inside the cave.

Bo slowly made his way down the rock face inside the cave using only the light that filtered in through the cave opening. It seemed to be just a single-room cave with only one way in and out. Once he made sure there was nothing there, Bo climbed out and waved for Jenny to join him inside the cave.

When she reached the cave, Bo told her of the branch he saw outside and that this probably wasn't the right cave, but he still wanted to build a fire inside to get a better look, just in case. Bo wandered outside and gathered some firewood and built the fire in the middle of the cave.

He then noticed several tunnels leading to different areas. Now, he thought, they may have found it!

Todd and JT arrived back at the camp and noticed that something had visited them while they were gone.

JT told Todd to stay close behind him. The two were walking around one of the tents when, without warning, a large bear stood up in front of them.

It was growling and not too happy that JT and Todd had walked up on it. JT could see that the bear had found their cooler and had been helping itself to the food the group had packed in the snow.

JT slowly began to back up. The grizzly, still on two feet, began to charge. Todd turned and began to run as fast as he could towards the trees with JT close behind.

The bear was chasing them, but now on all fours. Todd scampered up a tree, but JT didn't make it.

The bear was on JT and JT was fighting for his life. The heavy paws of the bear were smashing into JT's sides as he tried to play dead.

Suddenly, an arrow from above pierced the head of the giant. The bear stumbled back and fell over dead right there at the foot of the tree.

JT was battered and had several cuts and bruises, but was not seriously injured in the attack.

Todd screamed to JT, "Are you okay? Are you okay?"

Afraid to climb down from his perch, he just sat there waiting for a response from JT. JT slowly rolled over, still not realizing that the bear was dead.

When he saw the arrow that had completely gone in one side and was protruding a few inches out the other side of the bear's head, he got to his feet.

Todd, who was still yelling for JT to affirm that he was okay, now made his way back down the tree. He ran over to JT and put his arms around him.

JT, still a little stunned from the attack, looked down at the bear and told Todd, "See, I told you that you would get one next time."

JT put his arm around Todd and Todd helped him back to the campsite. They sat by the fire and JT checked himself over for missing limbs or fingers. He was relieved to find that they were all still there.

He looked at Todd and told him, "You saved my life!"

Bo wanted to venture deeper into the caves, but Jenny talked him out of it. She explained that the best thing to do was to set up the cameras and head back until tomorrow. Bo agreed and started putting out the fire.

They were making their way to the mouth of the cave

when the overwhelming smell crept deep into their nostrils. Bo pulled Jenny close as he hugged the rocks. It was dark and they didn't even know where the smell was coming from yet.

"Don't move a muscle," he whispered in her ear. The two stood frozen and plastered to the wall of the cave when the light was blocked by a shadow at the entrance. The beast made its way into the cave. It seemed to be just walking through when it stopped and began to look around.

Bo and Jenny were both holding their breath. The Bigfoot, satisfied it was alone, went through the middle of the three tunnels they had seen when the fire was burning.

They didn't move until several moments after the smell was gone. They quietly made their way out of the cave and into the woods.

They couldn't believe the thing just walked right past them!

Bo told Jenny to stay there while he went back to set up the camera. She argued that it would be faster if they both went, and he eventually gave in. They walked back to the line of trees. Then Bo made his way up one of the trees and placed the camera, aiming it directly at the mouth of the cave. They turned everything on and made their way back to a safe distance from the cave, where they stopped to rest.

They were both excited that they not only found what they believed was the home of the creatures, but were able to set up a camera.

"We've got it, baby," Bo said.

Jenny smiled back at Bo and responded, "We sure did."

They waited for a while before heading back, so they could rest and take in what they had just been through. Once they were ready, they began their hike back.

They didn't have any trouble navigating the rocks at the crossing and the trip back was uneventful.

When they got back, they were shocked to see JT with bandages wrapped around his arms and waist.

"What the hell happened to you?" Bo asked.

JT told them about the bear and how Todd saved his life.

Once they were sure that JT was okay, Bo and Jenny told them about finding the cave and how the Bigfoot walked right past them just a few feet away. There were only a couple of hours of light left and their food was gone again.

It was Todd who mentioned the dead bear and he and Bo went to where the bear was and carefully carved out enough food for the group's dinner. Bo was concerned that the bear would attract wolves and predators throughout the night, but it was too big to move and it just had to stay where it was.

Bo was proud of Todd for what he had done. He told him how brave he had been and Todd was happy that a man like Bo was so proud of him.

They walked back to the fire and cooked the best meal they had eaten in days. Bo put the rest of the meat in the cooler and packed it with what little snow was left. This time, he wrapped the cooler in duct tape to ensure they didn't lose it.

As darkness settled in, the group listened to the howls of what they were sure was the Bigfoot that was coming from a distance.

Bo noticed that JT's color changed to a pale white. JT complained that his side was bothering him, but assured them that he was okay. He just needed a good night's sleep and he would be just fine. They helped him to his tent, where he fell asleep in just minutes.

Jenny was worried about JT. He looked worse when they put him to bed than he did when they arrived back at camp.

The remaining three sat up for a while talking about their day.

Todd was still excited about the bear he had killed and wanted to make sure they heard every word. When they had finished listening to Todd's version of the story, they all went to bed, but it wasn't long before Jenny left her tent and joined Bo in his.

Chapter 8

The night turned to day and all four slept longer than usual. Todd was the first to wake up and notice that the day was beautiful. The normally cold mornings gave way to the now warmer one. Todd sat back and felt the warmth of the sun on his face. It was something that he missed over the past week. He hadn't realized that it was going to be so hard or dangerous to camp in the wilderness. Sure, he'd been camping in the past, but this wasn't a campsite surrounded by noisy patrons that most of us are used to. This was the wilderness! Mother Nature at her best. And Todd seemed to be enjoying every minute of it.

Of course, he was scared when the bear attacked, but now that it was over, he was glad to have had the experience. In a matter of one week's time, this boy had grown into a man. After all, he killed a giant grizzly bear and had seen Bigfoot with his own eyes. And if that didn't make him a man, nothing would. He looked up to

Bo and JT, and was proud of his sister for all she had done and experienced.

She had had the courage to continue when even Bo said they should pack it up. She, in his mind, was as much a hero as Bo or JT.

There was one thing that weighed heavily on his mind, though—the fact that he saved JT's life. Did he, he asked himself, or did JT save his?

Let's face it, JT made sure that Todd stayed behind him when they first saw the bear and if he really wanted to, JT surely could have outrun him to the tree.

Maybe JT saved his life by giving him time to climb the tree. If this was true, then JT must have had a lot of faith in him to shoot the bear or he most certainly would have been killed. He guessed they were both heroes. He and JT saved each other.

His thoughts were interrupted by the sound of the zipper on Bo's tent as Bo made his way out. He walked over to the fire pit and realized there was no fire burning.

He looked at Todd with a still sleepy look and one eye half closed, trying to shield them from the sun.

"You're slipping," he said to Todd, and he reached over and gave Todd a rough shake on the top of his head.

Todd smiled and said, "Don't you feel how warm it is out here?"

Bo looked up at the sky again and asked, "How do you plan to cook that bear meat?"

Todd smiled again and admitted he hadn't thought about cooking, he just knew it was warm enough that they didn't need to sit by the fire to stay warm.

Todd went to get some wood for the fire and Bo walked over to JT's tent and peeked in to check on his friend. JT was still asleep, but his color wasn't back to normal. Bo knew this was bad because if JT couldn't get up, he and Jenny would be unable to get the camera. He couldn't leave Todd here by himself and Jenny sure wouldn't let him go alone. What was he going to do now?

He thought about slipping away before she got up, but that idea was foiled as she made her way out of the tent.

"Good morning, sunshine," he said, as he rubbed what had grown into an almost full beard.

She smiled and kissed him softly on the cheek and said, "Good morning to you, too."

"So, how are we going to do this?"

Puzzled, she asked, "Do what?"

"Well," he responded, "we have to get the camera back and we can't leave JT and Todd here by themselves, so I guess I'll have to go alone."

"No way," she snapped. "If something happens to you out there, then we're sitting ducks here."

Bo knew she was right, but he still wanted to get his hands on that camera today and leave in the morning. He had no doubt that what they were looking for was on that camera.

"I don't think Todd is ready for a trip like this and I don't think he's ready to watch over JT either, so what do we do?" he asked again.

Jenny pondered for a long while when she finally said, "If you and I ran there and back, we would only be gone for about six or seven hours. JT and Todd would be fine for that long."

Bo scratched his head in deep thought, and then replied, "Listen, if those things do come back today and we're gone, they could kill those two with JT not up to par. And that's not a chance I'm willing to take. So, the bottom line is, it's either me by myself or not at all today!"

Jenny was visibly upset that Bo was being so demanding with his tone. "And what if JT isn't feeling better tomorrow either or the next day. Then what?"

Before Bo could answer, Todd came back with the wood for the fire.

"If you two want to go, then go," Todd insisted.

He could hear their entire conversation while gathering wood. Bo and Jenny were surprised that Todd had overheard them.

"It wasn't like you guys were whispering." Bo looked at Todd and spoke much softer than he had to Jenny.

"Look, buddy, it's not that I don't think you can handle yourself. I saw what you did to that bear. I just feel like our best bet is to let me run over there and back alone. You both have proven to me that you can handle yourselves. I just can't take that chance with JT."

Todd looked at Bo and said, "I understand, and so far, everything you've wanted to do has worked out pretty good. At least we're all still alive."

Bo looked at Jenny and asked, "Why can't you see it that way?"

"But," Todd continued, "this time I think you're wrong. You yourself said we should never be alone out here."

Bo carefully interrupted, "And with JT laid up in his tent, you would be alone. When there were four of us, it was easy. Now, there's only three."

JT slowly made his way out of his tent. Bo jumped up and helped him to the fire. JT had heard the entire conversation as well while lying awake in his tent.

"Look, guys," JT said, "I've known Bo for a while, and if anyone can make it there and back alone, it's him."

JT looked over at Jenny. "I know you'll worry every second he's gone." He then moved his attention to Todd. "You've been really brave with the bear and all, but you have to understand what he's saying. He could make it there and back a full hour faster by himself. I don't know about you two, but I'm ready to get the hell out of here."

Jenny looked over at Bo and asked him if this was really what he thought was best.

"It really is," he responded.

They all agreed that Bo would go alone today.

"It's ten thirty now," Bo said. "By the time we eat and I head out, it will most likely be noon. I should be back no later than six."

It was ten minutes after twelve when Bo had eaten, got his pack ready, and headed out to retrieve what he knew in his heart was all the proof they needed to prove the existence of a Bigfoot. As he walked through the thick brush, he looked over the beautiful mountains he had grown accustomed to. He began to worry about his friends. This was really the first time that Jenny wasn't safe by his side and he knew JT didn't look good.

When he reached the stream that was too high to cross the day before, he decided that now, by himself, he could probably make it across. The water had receded a little from before, so he started out across the stream.

Bo was surprised by the fact that the water was as shallow as it was, but the current proved to be strong when his foot slipped on a rock that rested at the bottom. In just a blink of an eye, Bo was pulled downstream as he struggled for something to grasp on to. He was tossed and turned violently as he was forced by the raging water to uncharted areas of the wilderness. The current had carried Bo to a pile of rocks and dumped him off. He was battered, bruised, and cold, but most of all, he was lost.

Back at camp, Jenny and Todd went to check on JT. He looked a little better now than he did this morning.

"How are you feeling?" she asked.

JT smiled and said, "If I felt any better, then we would have to throw a party."

"Oh, don't worry," she said. "When we get out of here, we're going to have the biggest party you've ever seen."

JT was actually feeling better and, with Jenny's help, he made his way to his feet and to the fire.

Todd was excited that JT was feeling better and offered him some coffee as he sat on a nearby log. Even though his body was weak, his mind was crystal clear. He could tell by the look on Jenny's face that she was worried about Bo.

JT reached over and put his hand on hers and assured her that Bo would be fine. Jenny knew that if anyone could go alone, and do it safely, it would be Bo, but still, there was that "what if" factor that raced through her mind.

Bo knew he had to start a fire so he didn't freeze to death. He walked up the steep embankment to a nearby wooded area and gathered up some wood and pulled his matches from the plastic baggy that he carried. It only took a few minutes and Bo was sitting next to a blazing fire.

He pulled out the map that he carried in the same

baggy and tried to find some landmark that would give him a clue as to where he was.

The fire was warm and he quickly dried off, but he was still unable to pinpoint where he was on the map. Bo knew that if he just followed the water upstream, he would eventually find his way back, but by the looks of it, he was going to have a hard time.

On both sides of the stream were steep cliffs that were chiseled out over thousands of years that he would have to climb first. Unfortunately, he didn't have the gear with him to make the climb. He would have to walk around the cliffs and he wasn't even sure how far of a hike that would be. He also knew he only had several hours of daylight left.

As Bo started putting out the fire to start his journey, he heard something walking through the leaves that scattered the ground in the thick woods. He ran to a nearby log that had recently fallen from a tree and hid and waited for whatever was coming towards him.

His heart raced as two men came walking through the brush.

The obviously older one of the two said, "Looks like whoever was here, we just missed them."

Bo slowly made his way out from behind the log where he was lying.

"I'm not gone yet," he said.

The two men seemed surprised as Bo walked towards them.

"Well, hello there, mister," the older one said. "My name is Chuck Barnes and this is my little brother, Stan." Chuck reached out to shake hands with Bo and noticed the cuts and bruised on him as they shook.

"What happened to you?" Chuck asked, not even giving Bo a chance to tell him his name.

"Well, I got swept down the stream," Bo answered. "I slipped on a loose rock and took a swim. My name is Bo."

The men finished their salutations and Bo asked if they could look at his map and tell him where they were.

"We're not on that map," he said, and he pointed a finger about a foot off the map and said, "We're about here."

Bo was surprised that he had gone so far. "That's some scary place that you took your spill," Chuck said. "Stan and I went out there about a year ago and we didn't stay long."

The comment made by Chuck really piqued Bo's interest, but he already knew what he meant by "scary" as he asked, "Why was it scary?"

"Oh, I don't know; a lot of noises in the night that we couldn't explain. I mean, we didn't see anything, but something sure wanted us gone, so we packed up and left real quick like."

"If you're hungry," Stan asked, "you can join us back at our camp for something to eat."

Bo pondered the question and knew that, based on where they said they were it would be getting dark about the time he made it back to the place he fell. And, with about another couple of hours from there, he would never make it back to camp. Jenny was going to worry herself sick.

Bo looked over at Stan and said, "I don't want to put you guys out, but I could use something to eat and maybe a place to lay my head."

"Right this way," Chuck insisted. "Besides," he

added, "we've got to get something to take care of those nasty cuts on your arms."

The men walked back into the heavy forest from which they came and Bo followed.

Back at camp, Jenny started making dinner, knowing that Bo would be getting back any time now. JT and Todd were playing a game of cards, with the deck they had purchased in town, to help pass the time.

After dinner was ready and Bo still hadn't come back, Jenny started to really worry about what may have happened to him.

JT looked over at Jenny and said, while he ate, "He's okay, you know. I would be lying if I said I wasn't worried, but he's okay."

She turned to him and he could see the tears she fought back as they welled up in her eyes.

"What if they found him? Even he wouldn't be able to fight those things off."

"You know," JT said in response, "one thing I've learned is when you don't know something for sure; it's always the worst case scenarios that seem to go through your head. But it never turns out to be as bad as what you're thinking. I mean, look, the odds of it being bad aren't as good as the odds of it being okay. For example, you've already made up your mind that he's dead or something. What if he got to the camera and the footage wasn't clear, or there wasn't anything at all? You know as well as me that he would wait until they came out to get the best shot possible."

This was supposed to make Jenny feel better, but it backfired on him. Now Jenny thought about the cave and how he probably went in to hide and get that shot he wanted.

JT reached over and put his arm around her and said, "Look, I know Bo is fine, you'll just have to trust him."

Jenny looked up at JT and nodded. "You're right," she said.

The three of them sat by the fire quietly until the darkness settled in on the camp and still no Bo.

When Bo and his newfound friends reached their camp, Chuck reached into his tent, grabbed the first aid kit, and fixed Bo up just as good as any doctor would.

"There you go. Good as new," Chuck said, as he finished wrapping Bo's arms. Bo thanked him for fixing him up and asked about their experiences in the area where he had fallen into the stream.

Chuck and Stan told Bo about what had happened a year ago and Bo listened intently. The experiences they described matched his almost verbatim.

Bo did tell a little of what they had heard, but left out all the sightings he, and mostly Jenny, had had.

"And they're still there?" Stan asked. He shivered as he asked it.

Bo pulled the map back out and asked if they knew the best way to the cave he had been headed to when the stream swept him away.

"You're only a couple of hours from there," Chuck said. "But you're not going to try to make it tonight, are you?"

"I wish I could," Bo said, while taking another bite of the fish the men had cooked up.

Chuck and his brother had been raised only a few

hours' drive from the main road that led into the mountains and they would visit out here as often as they could. They called it their "home away from home."

They explained that they thought the smoke they had seen from Bo's fire was the start of a forest fire, so they had gone to put it out, if they could.

Bo soon realized that the two men knew the area as well as anyone, so he listened as they told him what to look for until he got back to an area on the map.

The light soon faded to the darkness of night as they talked. The two men weren't used to visitors out here and Bo could tell that they were happy he was there, even if only for one night.

There was a clear sky and the stars filled the night sky. Bo lay awake and wondered what could possibly be going through Jenny's head right now as he stared up at the stars.

Jenny, back at their camp, was looking into the night sky as well.

Was Bo really okay?

She thought about all the things they had been through over the past week and all the fun they had been having, just being together. She realized at that moment, while looking at the brightest star in the sky, she was in love with Bo. And she could feel that he was looking at the same star at the exact same time. Calmness fell over her. She now felt and believed that Bo was okay and she would see him again.

Todd had already gone to bed and JT was still sitting with Jenny.

"You okay?" he asked her.

"Yeah," she paused while saying it, "I am."

It wasn't long after JT had made his way to his tent that the familiar howls could be heard in the woods. Jenny could tell that they were close, probably only a mile or so away. She wondered if Bo could hear the howls as well. The howls only lasted a few minutes and then they stopped.

Just minutes later, the campsite was under attack. Pine cones came flying through the air and smashed into the tents and the fire. Jenny ran to Bo's tent, where she sat watching through the partially unzipped flap as the bombardment continued.

It took only a few seconds, and again, the floor of the camp was littered with pine cones and the rocks that had been hurled at them.

Jenny knew they were being warned to leave the area. What she didn't know was that this was going to be their last warning.

Chapter 9

Bo woke up to the smell of bacon frying in a pan and coffee in the air. He slept well and knew he had gotten lucky yesterday when Chuck and Stan had gone out to investigate the smoke from his fire and found him.

"Hey, guys, thanks for everything you've done for me," he said as walked towards the fire where they already sat. "But I do have one favor to ask."

"Sure, whatcha need?" Stan asked.

"Look," Bo explained. "I have to go and find that cave. But I also know that Jenny will be out looking for me soon, and she really shouldn't be out there alone. If you wouldn't mind, and I hate asking after everything you guys have done for me already..."

"What would you like us to do?" Chuck asked.

"Well," Bo continued, "would you guys mind going to my camp to let them know I'm okay, while I go to the cave and get what I went after in the first place?"

"We would be happy to help you out," both men said simultaneously.

"What's up there at that cave that's so important anyway? That is, if you don't mind me asking?" Chuck asked.

Bo sat down at their makeshift table made of a tree stump from a tree that had been cut down years before. He didn't feel right sending the brothers out without telling them that they might have an encounter on their way.

Bo went on to tell the brothers everything that had happened over the past nine days. The brothers listened and when Bo had finished they sat open mouthed, not sure what to say.

Finally Stan asked if Bo was sure that the things he had seen were a Bigfoot.

"Without a doubt," Bo replied. "I have to get that camera today. If not, then what happened to Donald and JT was for nothing and we just wasted our time. And I can't let that happen."

Chuck, who was still surprised by what he had just heard, looked over at Stan and said, "You know, it could have been that Bigfoot thing that scared us out of there last year."

Bo interrupted, saying, "My guess is that it was. Everything you guys have said about what you heard is the same things we've been hearing."

The men ate breakfast and Bo told the brothers how to get to his campsite. When they had finished the three men took off into the woods. Bo went one direction and the brothers went in the other, guns in hand.

JT woke up to the familiar sound of arrows piercing into trees. He smiled as he stretched and realized that most of the soreness had gone.

JT climbed out of his tent and walked over to where Todd was practicing with his bow and watch quietly. Todd was completely unaware that JT was standing there as he finished off his quiver of arrows. When Todd turned he was happy to see JT standing there and obviously feeling much better.

"How are you feeling this morning?" Todd asked.

"Good, looks like you're getting the hang of that thing," JT responded. "I never really got a chance to thank you for killing that bear."

Todd was noticeably surprised by what he had just heard.

"You're thanking me? You could've outrun me and been up that tree. And I would have been the one who was on the ground. I should be the one thanking you."

"Look," JT said as he walked over to Todd and put an arm over his shoulder. "If I would have passed you, you would be dead. I didn't have the bow. But you came through and did what you had to to make sure we both survived. You saved my life by killing that bear and I'll never forget it."

It was then that they heard Jenny as she made her way from her tent.

And of course her first question was, "Did Bo make it back yet?"

JT assured her that it was still early and he was sure that Bo would be back with in the next few hours.

Jenny remembered the feeling she had the night before while looking at the northern star and she smiled as she responded, "I know, just thought…just maybe?"

Bo walked through the thick woods and took the shortcut that the brothers had told him about. He was happy to realize that in just a couple of hours he had reached the tree that he and Jenny had mounted the camera in. But to his surprise…the camera was gone!

With JT looking and feeling a lot better, Jenny informed him that she was going to look for Bo. JT knew deep inside that it really was a good idea. And he also knew it wouldn't do any good to argue with her about it.

He suggested that he and Todd join her, but she wouldn't have it. Jenny had decided to find him and not let another night go by with him stranded in the woods.

Jenny grabbed her pack and headed out to find Bo. She was careful to go exactly the same way as she and Bo had gone before. When she reached the stream, she followed it to the rocks that they had crossed before and carefully navigated her way across and headed towards the cave.

Her legs were tired and she felt like stopping for only a moment, but she knew she didn't have time for a break and she continued on.

Back at camp, JT and Todd sat by the fire playing their card game to help pass the time, when JT noticed about twenty yards away standing in the shadows of the forest was a figure of one of the beast. He looked closer to assure himself that his eyes weren't playing tricks on him.

There, just twenty yards or sixty feet from where they sat, was Bigfoot! It was just standing there watching as they played cards. JT's heart began to beat faster as he noticed that Todd hadn't seen the monster in the tree line yet. Where do you hide from a Bigfoot, JT questioned himself.

Todd was still bragging about the millions of dollars JT owed him from the last couple of hands as JT cut him off and told him to get up and walk slowly to his tent. JT was hoping that the old saying out of sight and out of mind would be the answer.

He followed Todd as they walked and they both crawled into the small tent.

After JT had told Todd what he had seen the two sat quietly and listened for any sounds. They could hear something walking around outside the tent when suddenly and without warning the top of the tent was ripped open, exposing the two men who sat helplessly inside.

They looked up to see what they assumed was the youngest of the three looking down at them. The smell was overwhelming as it glared into the tent growling. The noise was a loud and aggressive sound and the men were petrified as all they could do was watch.

Its head was large compared to the rest of its body and it was covered in a thick coat of dark brown hair that was matted in some spots.

JT grabbed Todd and tried holding him down as the beast reached in and pulled Todd out and through the roof of the tent by his neck.

Todd was dangled high in the air while his feet fluttered a few feet from the ground as the beast began to sniff around his head. Its wide nostrils flared out rapidly as it sniffed looking for a familiar scent. JT couldn't believe his eyes as the creature tossed Todd like a rag doll across the campsite.

Todd was dead from a broken neck before he even hit the ground.

Now the beast turned his attention to JT A lot of emotions raced through his head as he looked up at the monster. He couldn't believe that right there in front of him was the most elusive creature known to man and it had just killed Todd. And now it was about to grab him.

JT scrambled to the other side of the tent, to try and avoid sharing the same fate as Todd.

As the monster began to reach into the tent JT heard a gunshot ring out through the forest. The Monster stood up and looked over its shoulder as two more shots rang out. Both struck the giant in the chest.

JT could hear their impact as they hit.

The monster staggered back a couple of steps when again; two more shots came crashing into him. One cut into his shoulder and the other pierced the beast just below the chin and deep into its neck. The Bigfoot fell to one knee as one last shot rang out, this one hit the monster right between the eyes. It fell hard to the ground...dead! It had taken all it could.

JT still wasn't sure what was happening as he lay motionless at the bottom of the tent. In shock he raised his head and saw the two strangers making their way out of the forest. JT stood still surprised by the events that just took place and watched as the men ran in his direction.

He started to wave frantically to let them know he was still okay as he turned to see if Todd was still alive.

In what seemed like slow motion, JT could see the men drop to one knee and aim their rifles in his direction. He turned to look behind him and noticed the largest of the three monsters running towards him.

He didn't have time to duck the long arm that was swinging at his head. The blow sent JT hurling through the air.

The monster picked up its dead child and ran back towards the darkness of the woods. Chuck and Stan both got off a shot at the beast but assumed they missed because the beast showed no reaction. They ran as fast as they could to where JT landed.

When they arrived they heard JT say, "Check on the boy" as the last breath left his body.

Bo searched frantically for some clue as to where the camera had gone. He knew he was at the right tree that he had strapped it into about fifteen feet above the ground.

Could the Bigfoot have found the camera, he wondered. Bo started to question whether this was even the right tree. He searched high into some of the surrounding trees but found nothing.

"If the Bigfoot found it, what would he do with it?" he asked himself out loud. Probably throw it, but where, he wondered.

He began to look around, when a reflection of light hit his eyes. *Bingo,* he thought. He made his way through some thorny bush where the reflection had come from.

He reached deep in the brush and pulled out the camera, but was surprised to find it had been broken in two. Bo was angry as he cursed out loud at his misfortune, not thinking about a Bigfoot that may be just inside the cave just several yards away.

Jenny had made it to the spot where she and Bo, had once before began to start crawling when she heard Bo's voice from just over an outcropping of rocks.

Without thinking, she jumped to her feet and started sprinting towards the voice she heard. As she made her way to the sounds she wondered if he were okay or if maybe...he had been hurt and had been there all night.

While she ran, something suddenly grabbed her around the mouth and pulled her hard to the ground.

It was Bo! She turned and wrapped her arms around him tightly. "I thought you—" He put his hand back over her mouth and signaled her to look towards the cave.

At the mouth of the cave the largest of the Bigfoot creatures was laying the smaller, dead one on the rocks and looking curiously in their direction.

Jenny froze and Bo released her mouth signaling this time for her not to make a sound.

The couple crawled under the outcropped rocks and hid as the beast searched for the noises it had obviously heard.

The Bigfoot walked within several feet from where they where hiding but saw nothing. It sniffed around high in the air and seemed to know someone or something was there. It searched only a couple of minutes and when it was sure the coast was clear it made its way back to the corpse of the younger one and picked it up and disappeared into the mouth of the cave.

Bo wanted so badly to pull Jenny's lips against his and kiss the women he missed so badly, but they lay frozen for several minutes until they were sure the Bigfoot was gone.

After some time had passed, Bo signaled for Jenny to stay and he crawled towards the cave.

He wondered about the dead Bigfoot and how it died. As he crawled along on his belly he discovered a few drops of blood that was seemingly left by the larger beast

111

that just moments ago stood and sniffed in the air just a few feet from him and Jenny. He pulled off a piece of clean wrapping that his new friends used to wrap up his wounds from the day before and wiped up the blood in an attempt to collect some blood samples.

With the blood sample safely in his pocket, he turned and made his way back to Jenny, signaling her to follow him out of the area. When they had made it to an opening near the stream and far from the cave, Bo grabbed her and puller her tightly against him.

"I missed you," he said.

She squeezed back and told him how she thought he was dead as the tears slowly rolled down her face.

Bo pulled away, still holding her arms, and asked about JT and Todd. She explained that Todd and JT were just fine and how it was JT who told her she should go look for him.

"What happened to you last night? I was worried sick," she said.

Bo scratched his head as he told her about the spill he took in the stream and how he met Chuck and Stan. "In fact," he continued, "they are probably sitting with JT and Todd as we speak."

It was about that time when Chuck and Stan made their way out of the woods and to the clearing on the other side of the stream.

Bo, puzzled, looked over and figured that JT and Todd must have insisted that the brothers go out and find Jenny. They all walked downstream where Jenny and Bo made the crossing to the other side. When they reached the brothers Bo reached out to shake their hand and thank them for all they had done.

The look on their faces told Bo that something was wrong.

"What is it?" Bo asked. Stan lowered his head as Chuck began to explain to Bo what had happened at the campsite.

Jenny, who overheard the conversation, screamed out, "No, no! It must have been a different campsite that they had walked up on."

"Ma'am," Chuck said softly while holding his hat in his hands, "I really wish it was the wrong camp."

Bo walked over to Jenny and held her close as she cried out with her head buried deep in his chest.

"If you want," Chuck said softly, "you two are welcome to stay at our campsite tonight."

Bo thought about how it was he, who talked everyone into believing that the giants weren't dangerous and he carried the blame squarely on his shoulders.

"Yeah," Bo finally answered. "That's probably a good idea."

Bo and Jenny followed the brothers into the woods and back to their campsite.

When they arrived to the camp Bo took Jenny to one of the tents and they lay holding each other tight, but not talking. The roller coaster of emotions Jenny had gone through today was too much for her to handle. It was too much for anyone to handle for that matter.

From the worry she felt for Bo being lost in the forest, to the happiness she felt that JT was feeling so much better, to the fear when she heard Bo's voice near the cave, to the joy when she realized he was okay, and finally the terror to hear that she had lost a brother and a friend. She quickly fell asleep and Bo crawled out of the tent to talk to the brothers about what had happened.

Bo was much better at hiding his emotions as he listened to the story the brothers told him.

Stan explained that Chuck had killed one of the beasts with a bullet between the eyes, and how they were sure they hit the bigger one, but it didn't act like it was hit. Using low-caliber weapons, they were surprised that they managed to kill the younger one.

Bo reached in his pocket remembering the blood he had found on the rock near the cave.

"You hit it," Bo said. "You killed one and hit the other."

"How do you know that?" Stan asked.

"Look," Bo answered. "I found some blood earlier on the ground after the big one was looking for us by the cave."

He showed them the blood-stained wrap. "In fact," Bo continued, "I bet that's why it didn't spend a lot of time looking for us. It was hurt and wanted to get the other one inside the cave."

Chuck and Stan listen as Bo talked, when suddenly Bo's facial expression changed.

"What time is it?" Bo asked.

"It's about seven thirty, why?" Chuck asked.

Chuck could see the look in Bo's eyes.

"I'm going back to finish those things off," Bo insisted as he grabbed his back pack and started walking back towards the cave.

"Wait," Chuck said as he stepped in front of Bo and put his hand up to stop him. "I don't think that's such a good idea, we're all safe here out of their territory. And don't you think she's been through enough today? Come on, man," he continued. "Her brother and a friend were killed today and she thought you were dead most of the day."

Chuck pleaded with Bo to stay.

Bo stopped and fell to his knees and began to sob as the emotions overwhelmed the control he had. He thought about his old friend and his new friend, about all the fun they have had these last nine days. And how Chuck was right, Jenny had been through enough.

Soon, even Chuck and Stan had tears in their eyes as well.

Bo walked over and watched Jenny as she slept. He could tell that she was dreaming about happier times. After watching her for a while he walked back over to where the brothers were and thanked them for all that they'd done for him and his friends.

Bo asked about the bodies. Stan told him that they had buried them in shallow graves so nothing would get to them. Chuck added that they would be happy to show him where in the morning. Bo knew he couldn't be mad about it because he had done the same thing with Donald's body. But it felt different now that it was someone he knew so well.

Bo reached into his pack and pulled out his broken camera that he retrieved from the thorny brush.

He stood looking at it when he said, "You know, guys, if this camera hadn't been broken my friends wouldn't have died for nothing. We would have proof that these things are out there."

As Bo stared at the broken camera and wondered, *What if...* He noticed the video card was still in place. It was just a small chip that held everything that the camera saw over a twelve-hour span.

Bo quickly ran over and grabbed Jenny's camera and placed the video card in it and turned it on. He fast-forwarded until he saw movement.

Then he would rewind it and play it at normal speed. After going through the process several times with deer and a bear on one occasion, he was surprised and couldn't believe his eyes.

Two of the monsters walked out of the cave and returned a while later. The image on film was clear and there was plenty of light. As the three men watched the tape they could clearly make out the larger beast look up at the camera and walk over to it to investigate. Its large hand reached high in the tree and simply plucked the camera from where Bo had placed it.

They watched as the Bigfoot looked into the camera and sniffed trying to figure out what it was. Then static as the Bigfoot broke the camera in half.

Bo sat dumbfounded as bittersweet excitement ran through his veins. He only wished JT and Todd were here to enjoy it with him.

Chuck and Stan were excited for Bo and what he had found.

"If proof is what you wanted, you got it!" Stan said as he laughed.

"This is incredible," Bo said as he started towards Jenny's tent to show her the footage. Jenny had been awakened by the excitement and was making her way out of the tent as Bo approached.

She looked confused and asked what was going on.

"We got it," Bo said. "We got it on film."

Jenny smiled softly as she watched the tape. She was happy to have proof, but she knew it wasn't worth it with the loss of her brother and friend.

The group sat up for a while telling stories about JT and Todd. They talked about the fun that they had had on this trip—up until today anyway.

Bo mentioned how proud their fallen friends would be with the footage they had gotten.

It wasn't long before their tired eyes began to give out on them and they all made their way to their tents.

Bo and Jenny held each other close in the tent that the brothers had lent them.

Bo knew he had to go back to their campsite in the morning and look for any more evidence that the Bigfoot may have left behind, but wasn't sure it was a good idea that Jenny went along. She had already been through so much.

He softly ran his finger along her cheek to wipe away the tears that still ran slowly down her cheek.

"You should head back to town in the morning," Bo said softly.

"What about you?" she asked.

"I'm going to go back to camp and get our things and I have to get my Jeep, but I'll meet you in town tomorrow."

Jenny wasn't happy with the fact that Bo was planning to go back, and she sharply replied, "If you go, then I'm going with you."

Bo had expected her to say just that, and responded, "You could go, but I need you to get the footage and all the other evidence to a safe place."

Jenny hated the idea and told him that he couldn't go alone.

"I won't, I'm going to ask Chuck to go with me while Stan takes you back to town. Will that be okay with you?"

Jenny was already mentally strained and gave in to the idea as long as Chuck went with him.

The night was filled with the normal sounds that they missed so badly. They held each other tight and didn't talk anymore the rest of the night. It wasn't long before they were fast asleep.

Chapter 10

Sunday October 23rd 2006
Day 10

Bo lay awake in his tent wondering about how he was going to tell Sarah about JT. He knew she wasn't going to take it well. She was ready to settle down and start her family, and JT was the one she planned to do it with.

He also thought about Todd and how much he meant to Jenny. All the thoughts swirled around in his head as he tried to make some sense out of all that had happened.

Bo could hear the zipper on the door from the other tent as it opened and Chuck made his way out.

Quietly getting up, Bo joined Chuck by the fire. It was still dark and the normal night sounds still filled the air. To Bo this meant that Bigfoot was territorial. He grinned as he thought how much of an expert he had become on the whole Bigfoot phenomenon.

Bo asked Chuck about going back to the campsite with him this morning and told him about how dangerous it could be.

Chuck smiled and looked forward to helping his new friend.

When Stan woke up they let him in on their plan. He too agreed to do his part.

Bo knew it was important to let the authorities know about the bodies and to tell them and only them about what had happened. He stressed that he didn't want the press to know anything yet. They still had to develop a plan as far as the press was concerned.

Chuck and Bo had all their gear ready and the campsite was packed up except for the tent that Jenny slept in, and she didn't get up until ten.

When she got up she could tell by the gear sitting away from everything else that Chuck must have agreed to Bo's request. She made her way to Bo and wrapped her arms around him and begged him to be careful.

Then she warned Chuck with a halfhearted smile that he had better take good care of Bo.

Chuck assured her that they would be just fine.

Bo pulled her close and kissed her. "I'll see you tonight," he said.

She smiled softly at him and said again, "Be careful out there."

Bo grabbed his gear and he and Chuck disappeared into the woods on their way back to the campsite that Bo and Jenny had called home for over a week.

Jenny watched the men until they were out of sight.

Stan had already taken down the last tent and was packing it up when he asked Jenny if she was ready to go.

She nodded and they started making their way to the truck. Jenny and Stan arrived at his truck about an hour later and loaded everything into the back and they began to make their way back to town.

Bo and Chuck made good time getting to the campsite.

When they arrived, Chuck was surprised to see that the Bigfoot had returned and ransacked the camp again.

"It didn't look like this yesterday when we left it," Chuck informed Bo. All the tents had been uprooted and completely destroyed. Rocks and large sticks littered the campsite. It was as if the monsters thought someone was in the tents and were trying to get to them.

"It looks like it was a good thing you guys didn't stay here last night," Chuck said as he kicked around a small pile of sticks.

Bo was digging around the mess looking for the small camera they had used to take pictures of the dead deer they had found as well as pictures of themselves on their trip.

"Yeah, I think you're right. This could have been bad last night," Bo replied.

Bo looked over at Chuck and asked, "Where did you... You know... The bodies?"

Chuck knew what Bo was trying to ask and he pointed to a small clearing just past a small row of trees.

Bo walked over and was glad to see that the graves were undisturbed. He looked down at the graves and told JT and Todd about what they had found. He explained that they would be proud to know that they got the footage. After talking softly for several minutes to the shallow graves where the bodies had been put the day before, He went back to continue his search for the camera and anything else he could find.

Chuck watched the trees for any unwanted visitors while Bo searched.

Bo started filling a bag that he had brought with them with personal items belonging to JT and Todd. He put in a wallet that belonged to JT and the deck of cards he found spread out on the ground where JT and Todd were sitting when the attack started.

His eyes began to swell up with tears as he loaded item after item and remembering something about each as he put them in the bag.

When he was done he took a moment to regain his composure and walked over to Chuck and asked, "See anything?"

"No, but something doesn't feel right," Chuck responded.

Bo gripped the rifle that he had borrowed from Stan. He realized that Chuck was referring to the total silence in the woods. He hadn't noticed it because he had gotten used to it.

"They're out there. We had better get going. It's a long walk back to my Jeep," Bo said.

Chuck was ready to go even before Bo made the suggestion.

"You got everything you need?" Chuck asked as he looked back at Bo.

"Yep, let's get out of here," Bo replied.

The two men headed back into the thick forest on their way to Bo's Jeep.

Stan and Jenny had been driving for a while without saying a word, when Jenny broke the silence, asking, "You think they'll be okay?"

"Jenny, you got a good man there and I'm sure that they'll be just fine," Stan replied. He continued saying, "Nobody knows those woods better than Chuck, and with those two out there together there really isn't much that can happen to them."

Jenny looked over at Stan and thanked him for reassuring her and for everything he'd done to help them.

Jenny sat up straight in her seat and turned to Stan, asking if he had any idea what he and his brother had done the day before.

"What do you mean?" he asked.

"When you guys killed that Bigfoot," she said, then waited for an answer.

His expression changed to a sad look as he explained that they didn't care about that; the only thing they were doing was trying to save her brother and friend.

Jenny reached over and put her hand on his shoulder and said. "I know, but no one has ever killed one of those things before."

Stan looked back and smiled as he responded. "No one will believe it after the other one ran off with it."

"Yeah, but Bo and I know where he carried it off to."

Stan looked at Jenny confused and asked, "What are you getting at?" He thought for a minute that she may have wanted to go get it right now.

"Listen," she said, "when this gets out, there are going to be a lot of people out looking for those things. But you guys will always be known as the first people to ever kill a Bigfoot."

She could tell by the blank look on his face that notoriety nor fame seemed to interest him. So she added, "You two could get rich off this."

He wondered how they would get rich when all they did was try to save someone's life and they didn't even succeed at that.

"They're going to write books and want you two to do

interviews and all kinds of things like that. Maybe even a movie," she added.

"Look, I don't want any part of all that stuff. We're just a couple of country boys who went camping and got caught up in something that... Well, we didn't ask to get caught up in."

Jenny explained that Patterson was just a rodeo cowboy himself and he had gotten the best piece of evidence of all time. Until now. she thought.

The conversation went on until they had finally reached the motel that they had earlier decided was the best place to meet up with Bo and Chuck later.

Stan went inside and paid for two rooms that were side by side and gave one key to Jenny.

The motel was small, quiet and actually quite nice. It only had about fifteen rooms and sat just off the main road. Jenny went into her room and was glad to get a real shower and sleep in a real bed. It had been awhile since she had been able to have such a luxury.

She and Stan had both gotten a shower and Stan went next door and knocked on the door marked room number nine. She invited him in and they decided that this was the time to call the local sheriff.

She picked up the phone and began to dial, when she stopped and hung the phone back on the cradle.

"What's wrong?" Stan asked as he looked at Jenny confused.

"It might be better if we just go to the sheriff's office in person. How am I going to explain this over the phone? They'll just think it's a prank call."

Stan agreed, so they left the room and headed out to find the sheriff's office.

The terrain was rough and Chuck decided to stop and take a break. "You all right?" Bo asked.

"Oh yeah," Chuck replied as he took in several deep breaths.

Chuck had been looking over his shoulder the entire hike from the campsite, and was beginning to get nervous.

"Can you feel it? It's been watching us the whole way," Chuck asked.

"Yeah, I know, but we got to keep moving. We still have to go a couple more hours before we reach the Jeep, and if we stop, we're just sitting ducks," Bo replied.

As the men started to get up to continue their hike, they heard the sound of something running fast through the woods.

They readied their rifles, watching for it to make its move at them. But it seemed to run right past them from only fifteen or twenty yards inside the thick woods. Neither man saw the beast, but it was heavy and fast and they both knew that the monster was close.

They started making their way with their rifles chest high. They fought their way through the thick brush and tall trees, watching and listening for any more signs of the beast.

After going on for only a couple hundred yards, Bo stopped suddenly. They both dropped to their belly and scanned the forest just ahead.

"You see it?" Bo whispered.

Chuck studied the area close and asked softly, "Where?"

Bo carefully and quietly made his way back to where Chuck was and pointed to a dark figure that was hiding in the brush just ahead of them about sixty feet or so.

"This damn thing is setting us up for an ambush," Bo said as he realized the true nature of what was happening.

Chuck finally saw the dark outline and agreed that it wasn't just a stump or anything like that, it was the Bigfoot and Bo was right, it was setting them up.

"We can't keep going in this direction," Bo said.

Chuck looked around and began to get his bearings when he remembered a path that ran parallel to them not too far away. He explained to Bo that the path would be much easier to walk, but it would take them a little out of the way and would probably take them about an hour longer to reach the Jeep.

"Well we can't go this way. That's for sure," Bo exclaimed.

Chuck took the lead as they made their way towards the path. Bo began to think about how smart this thing was. It could have attacked them when it ran by, but it probably knew they had the rifles. It just lay hiding in the brush and was going to attack them as they walked by it. *This must be the same tactic it uses on deer. It probably hides and grabs the deer's leg as it walks by.* This would at least explain how all the dead deer with the missing liver had one and sometimes two broken legs.

It was hunting Bo and Chuck just like it did the unsuspecting deer that would simply walk upon it.

They soon reached the path and Bo listened closely and scanned the area. He was happy to hear the normal sounds of the forest and if he had learned one thing, it was that if the other animals in the forest weren't scared, then he shouldn't be either.

They walked slowly, as they made their way down the path.

When the forest suddenly got quiet again and hundreds of bird seemed to take flight all at once. Bo and Chuck looked frantically for a place to hide.

Chuck noticed a tree that was hollow and they ran inside to take cover. There was plenty of room for the two men inside the tree and they sat quietly and waited. Bo looked around the inside and noticed a single beam of light that filtered in through a hole a few feet up inside the massive tree. He climbed up the inside of the tree and looked out through the hole.

He could see most of the path from his hiding place, and it was only a few seconds when he watched the Bigfoot step out of the trees and stop on the path.

Bo reached down and patted Chuck on the shoulder, letting him know that it was there and not to make a sound.

Bo watched as the Sasquatch looked up and down the path in both directions, no doubt looking for them. It stood with its head high in the air, taking in the smells that lingered around the forest. It sniffed a few times and then looked directly in their direction.

Bo wondered if they should run out shooting and try to kill the beast or just stay put while trying to sneak around it. It looked hard in Bo's direction and had obviously picked up on their scent. But he didn't think that it had seen them.

Bo felt that this was the only one hunting them and the female was probably still back at the cave watching over the body of the younger one.

The beast took several steps in their direction and again it began to sniff high in the air. Bo could feel Chuck shaking and only hoped the Bigfoot didn't hear it.

After a few minutes the monster walked over the path and continued its search elsewhere. They stayed hidden for a while and figured this was the best place to take the much needed break.

Once the forest filled with its normal sounds the men headed on towards the Jeep.

Jenny and Stan pulled up to the sheriff's office and walked inside. The office was small, with only three people inside. The place reminded Stan of the old westerns and how the sheriff's office looked in the movies. But he kept his thoughts to himself and they walked up to the women at the desk and asked for the sheriff.

"What's the nature of your visit?" the lady asked.

"Well," Jenny pondered a second before answering, "it's a long story and I hope you're not going to make me tell it twice."

The lady looked Jenny and Stan over for a moment, and then looked over her shoulder at a man sitting at a desk reading a newspaper. "Larry!" the lady yelled across the room. "Some people are here to see you."

The sheriff didn't look at all like what she expected. She envisioned an older man, heavy, and probably smoking a cigar. But he wasn't anything like that. He was a younger man in his lower thirties, clean shaven and well groomed.

He got up and walked across the office to where Jenny and Stan were standing and held out his hand to Stan. Stan shook the sheriff's hand as the sheriff introduced himself. "Hello, I'm Sheriff Stevens. What can I help you with?"

Jenny explained that it was a long story and they should probably sit down in a quiet place.

Sheriff Stevens looked puzzled and waved for them to follow him to a nearby room, where they all sat down.

Jenny introduced herself and Stan and started telling the entire story from the top. Sheriff Stevens listened patiently, and when Jenny had finished he sat back in his chair and stared out the window for a long while, not saying anything.

"That's quite a story," the sheriff said as he put his arms on the table and leaned in towards Jenny.

"I have proof," Jenny said. She didn't think that the sheriff believed what she had told him.

The sheriff sat back in his chair with an intrigued look on his face. "Okay, you've piqued my interest. What kind of proof do you have?"

Jenny reached in her bag and showed the sheriff the footage that showed the Bigfoot reaching into the tree and grabbing the camera.

The sheriff again sat back in his chair and this time Jenny could tell that he believed every word. He then began asking questions.

"You mean to tell me that you still have friends still out there with this thing running around? And what about the bodies of the three dead men?"

Stan quickly jumped in, saying, "We buried them in shallow graves to keep the wild animals away from them."

Jenny was horrified by the thought of wild animals getting at her brother and had to fight back the tears as she informed the sheriff that everything they had said was the truth.

The sheriff sat thinking about a game plan, and then said, "Here's what we're going to do, I want you two to go back to your rooms and wait for your friends. I'm going to get some people together and meet you there at six o'clock in the morning and we'll go out there and get your brother and your friend. Then we'll look around and see if we can find the Bigfoot. If your friends aren't back in a few more hours, you call me."

Jenny knew it was getting late and Bo and Chuck should be back soon, so she agreed and she and Stan began to leave, when Stan stopped and looked back at the sheriff and said, "Bo asked me to tell you not to get the press involved yet. He wants to wait until we are all together to do that."

"Look, I've only got two deputies here and I think we're going to need a few more. I'll tell them not to talk about it, but I can't make any guarantees."

Stan nodded in agreement and he and Jenny made their way out the door.

The lady from behind the desk and the deputy who was there walked into the room where the sheriff still sat looking out the window. "What was that all about?" the lady asked.

The sheriff, who was still a little haunted by what he had just seen on the camera, looked up and told the others, "This is going to put our little town on the map."

The sheriff ordered the deputy to take a drive out to where Jenny had said the Jeep was and to let him know if he found it.

The deputy, still having no idea what was going on, left quickly in search of the Jeep.

He then asked the desk clerk to call the neighboring

county and see if they could call in their chopper tomorrow. Then he started making calls himself, trying to form a posse to try and track down the Bigfoot the next day.

As Stan and Jenny got in the truck, they saw the deputy running out to his car and racing off down the road.

"Do you think he believed us?" Stan asked as he started the truck.

"Oh yeah," she said. "He believed us."

It took Bo and Chuck a little longer to reach the road that the Jeep was parked on, but they were glad that they had finally made it. They had walked for a couple of miles when Bo spotted the Jeep, parked just about a half mile from them.

"There it is," Bo said, and the two men started walking faster.

When they were almost to the Jeep, Bo reached in his pocket and pulled out the key. Suddenly from out of nowhere the monster burst out and rammed hard into the side of the Jeep as if it was trying to tackle it.

It lowered its massive body and reached under the side of the Jeep and lifted it high in the air, flipping the vehicle completely onto its side. The two men were shocked at what they witnessed. They stood frozen as the beast stood and turned in their direction.

It looked at the men snarling and growling while pounding hard on its chest. Bo realized that it didn't want them to leave anymore, it wanted them dead.

The men turned and started running as fast as they could down the road in the opposite direction.

The Bigfoot seemed to give them a head start, then it started chasing after them. Its strides were long and it ran fast as it began to gain on them.

Bo knew they were in a lot of trouble, and then he saw a vehicle driving towards them up the road. The two men started waving their arms frantically in the air in hopes to get the driver's attention.

It was the deputy the sheriff had sent out to find the Jeep.

At this point all the deputy could see was the two men running down the middle of the road carrying rifles. He slammed on his brakes, causing the car to spin sideways.

The deputy jumped out of the car, pulling his revolver and aiming it in the direction of the two men. It was then that he saw why they were running.

He quickly jumped back into the car and forced it in reverse and started driving towards the men. When he reached them he again slammed on the brakes and the men jumped in.

As he stared to drive off the Bigfoot smashed its fist hard into the trunk of the police car, causing the lid to fly open. He sped off, leaving the beast standing in the middle of the road alone and frustrated.

It had gotten so close, but it missed its prey.

The deputy was shaken by what he had just seen and asked, "What the hell was that thing?"

Chuck yelled back, "Just drive!"

"How do I call this in?" the deputy asked himself out loud.

Bo and Chuck were worn out and exhausted after what they had just been through.

Chuck looked over at Bo and smiled as he said, "Well, we made it."

Bo smiled back and said, "That was crazy, did you see that thing's face?"

The two men were able to laugh now that they were in the safety of the car speeding down the road away from the creature.

The deputy, still questioning what he had just seen, decided that it would be better if he called the sheriff from his cell phone instead of using the radio that someone else could hear.

He dialed the number to Sheriff Stevens's cell phone and waited for an answer.

"Hello," a voice said on the other end.

"Larry, this is Dave and you're not going to believe this, but, I just saw something. I'm not really sure what it was, but it was big!"

"Listen, Dave, did you find the Jeep?" the sheriff asked, cutting him off. "No, not yet," Dave responded. "But I found these two guys running down the road being chased by... Well, I guess it was a Bigfoot."

"Is one of them named Bo?" the sheriff asked.

Dave looked back at the two men and asked if either of them was Bo, then handed Bo the phone when he told him that that was his name.

"This is Bo," he said as he spoke into the phone.

"I'm glad you're okay. This is Sheriff Stevens and I just wanted you two to know that your friends stopped in to see me today. Listen, have my deputy take you to your Jeep and I'll see you in the morning. Jenny will fill you in on the details."

Bo paused as he told the sheriff about his Jeep and asked if it was okay if the deputy took him to the motel instead.

"No problem, Bo. Just put the deputy back on the phone and make sure you guys get lots of rest tonight."

Bo thanked the sheriff and handed the phone back to the deputy. The deputy and the sheriff talked for a little longer while Bo and Chuck both nodded off in the backseat.

They pulled up to the motel and the deputy woke them up.

By now the sheriff had called Jenny's room and let her know that Bo and Chuck were safe and on their way to the motel.

Jenny and Stan sat outside on chairs from their room waiting for them to arrive. They quickly made their way to the police car as it pulled up.

Jenny jumped into Bo's arms when he climbed out of the cruiser and he held her tight while he planted a big kiss on her.

"I was so worried," Jenny said as she held him.

"I know," he said, "but it's all over now."

Bo looked at Jenny with a look of despair in his eyes and told her that there was one more thing he had to do.

"What's that?" Jenny asked.

"I have to call Sarah and tell her about JT."

Bo followed Jenny to their room and after dropping all the bags that he had been carrying all day he fell hard in the soft chair and sat for several minutes with his eyes closed.

He was looking for the best way to tell Sarah about JT—if there *was* a best way to tell her, he thought.

He reached over and pulled the phone up on his lap and began dialing the number. She answered and he explained that there was an attack in the woods and that JT didn't make it.

Jenny could hear Sarah screaming through the receiver from across the room. He talked to Sarah for about twenty minutes and explained the whole story to her. He also told her that he would handle all the details about getting his body home.

Of everything Bo had done over the past ten days, this had been, by far, the hardest.

After Bo had hung up the phone, he told Jenny about the Jeep and all the things that happened today.

They ordered pizza and discussed with the others the plan for tomorrow. Bo was tired and after Chuck and Stan returned to their room, Bo lay down on the soft bed.

Bo fell asleep fast as Jenny rubbed his back, and she soon followed.

Chapter 11
The Conclusion

Six o'clock came early and as he had promised, Sheriff Stevens knocked on Bo and Jenny's door. Jenny answered the door and found the sheriff holding a box of doughnuts in his hands, flanked by his two deputies.

"I figured you folks might be hungry."

Jenny invited the men in and went next door to get Chuck and Stan. The sheriff and Bo got acquainted and soon everyone was in the room.

The sheriff quickly went over the game plan for the day and asked if anyone had other suggestions to make sure everyone would be safe.

Everyone agreed that the plan was fine and they soon got up and went on their way to the campsite.

The sheriff stopped and picked up four more men for the trip.

Jenny felt safe with what were now ten men, who all but one were carrying high-powered rifles. The other man was carrying a gun loaded with tranquilizers, in hopes that they wouldn't have to kill another one.

It wasn't long before they had reached the campsite.

The first thing they had to do was to get a helicopter out there and take the three bodies back to town.

There was plenty of room by the creek to land one.

Bo took Jenny for a small hike, accompanied by several other people, while they dug up the graves and removed the bodies. They watched as the helicopter took off and flew out of sight.

They searched the campsite and surrounding area for any evidence. But they came up with only a few hairs and some footprints.

Bo led the party to the cave and several men went inside while Bo, Jenny, Chuck and Stan were asked to stay outside and wait. The men emerged about an hour later and told the sheriff that all they could find was three piles of brush that they assumed were used for bedding to keep them off the hard rocks. But there was no Bigfoot to be found.

Bo looked at the sheriff and said, "These things are smart, I bet they knew we would be back and left in the night. If you could track them somehow, you could follow them. But my guess is they went up high in the mountains, where it would be hard to track them."

The sheriff laughed softly and said, "Yeah, I was thinking the same thing. There's no reason to stay out here any longer."

After spending most of the day in the forest, they packed it up and left.

The sheriff and several volunteers searched for a few more days but came up with nothing more than what they found the first day. The four who were left went back to their normal lives, or at least as normal as they could make it.

The funerals for JT and Todd were held at the same church and at the same time. There were a lot of people who showed up to pay their respects. Most of them Jenny or Bo had never met and they just assumed that they were Bigfoot enthusiasts. Chuck and Stan showed up. And the four of them, along with Sarah, went out to eat afterwards. They all told stories about the two men, but none were more touching than when Chuck told Sarah what JT's last words were.

"'Check on the boy,'" Chuck said. "Even when he lay almost dead himself, all he wanted was for us to check on Todd."

There wasn't a dry eye at the table. The night ended with a lot of tears and good-byes.

Sarah went back to Southern Oregon and continued teaching. She told her class often about the stories the group had told to her. Her students always listened intently. It seemed to her that the students in her class listened better than the adults she had told.

Chuck and Stan turned down almost every request to do interviews. They did, however, do a piece on the outdoors cable channel and told just their part of the story. That particular episode received its highest rating ever. The brothers always spoke well about their new friends and on occasions they all got together for dinner.

Bo and Jenny became celebrities in the Bigfoot community. They spoke together at Bigfoot conventions and even went on expeditions into the wild on a few occasions. But neither of them ever saw the creature again. And that was just fine with them.

It was one year to the day that the adventure ended,

October 23, 2007, that Bo and Jenny had gotten married. It was a small and private ceremony. Bo chose not to use a best man. Instead, he had a picture of JT and Todd blown up and stood it where the best man would have stood. It was a picture that Jenny took of the two men standing next to their snowman. There wasn't a dry eye in the entire church.

Of all the evidence that they had collected, the best by far was the footage. The blood came back from testing and was said to not be from humans and of unknown origin.

The skeptics figured it was from some wild animal and had simply broken down over time. All the still photos taken of the deer really weren't proof of anything. But the believers felt that it did explain and confirm in some cases what the diet of the Bigfoot was.

The footage, much like the 1967 footage by Patterson, had been put through the wringer by skeptics. Most skeptics believed it was a man in a monkey suit. But no one could figure out how a man could reach so high in a tree and grab the camera.

The Bigfoot community was excited by the footage and, to them anyway, it became the most famous piece of evidence to prove the existence of Bigfoot. Some scientist who viewed the footage began to change their minds about the beast. They said there was no way to make those facial expressions in a suit. And the eyes were impossible to fake.

The deaths of JT and Todd were officially ruled caused by animal attack. Even though neither was bitten or clawed.

There had been a lot of skeptics that became believers after looking at what Bo and Jenny had collected.

Bo gives this piece of advice to every one he talks to during public speaking: "Don't try to hunt these things. If you come across one, turn and run away. They will give you plenty of warning, and you should listen to them when they do."

The most asked question to Bo, Jenny, Chuck or Stan is, "What happened to the dead one?"

They all give the same answer, "The big one just took it and ran, and I don't know where it ran to."

THE END

Lightning Source UK Ltd.
Milton Keynes UK
UKOW050609031211

183079UK00001B/47/P